Animals in Heaven?

Animals in Heaven?

✦

Catholics Want to Know!

Recognizing divine providence at work in creation

Susi Pittman

iUniverse, Inc.
New York Bloomington

iUniverse books may be ordered through booksellers or by contacting:

iUniverse
1663 Liberty Drive
Bloomington, IN 47403
www.iuniverse.com
1-800-Authors (1-800-288-4677)

Because of the dynamic nature of the Internet, any Web addresses or links
contained in this book may have changed since publication and may no longer be
valid. The views expressed in this work are solely those of the author and do not
necessarily reflect the views of the publisher, and the publisher hereby disclaims
any responsibility for them.

Excerpts from the English translation of the Catechism of the Catholic Church for
use in the United States of America © 1994, United States Catholic Conference,
Inc.—Libreria Editrice Vaticana. Used with permission.

All scripture quotations taken from the Catholic Edition of the Revised Standard
Version of the Bible, © 1965, 1966, by the Division of Christian Education of the
National Council of the Churches of Christ in the United States of America. Used
with permission. All rights reserved.

ISBN: 978-1-4401-7725-5 (sc)
ISBN: 978-1-4401-7726-2 (ebook)
ISBN: 978-1-4401-7727-9(hc)

Library of Congress Control Number: 2009936707

Printed in the United States of America

iUniverse rev. date: 10/30/2009

Declaration

I make my unconditional submission to the official teachings of the Magisterium of the Holy Roman Catholic Church, the living, teaching office whose authority is exercised in the name of Jesus Christ.

The Magisterium teaches us from sacred tradition and sacred scripture, to which nothing new can be added.

It is this Magisterium's task to preserve God's people from deviations and defections and to guarantee them the objective possibility of professing the true faith without error.[1]

I am the good shepherd; I know my own and my own know me, as the Father knows me and I know the Father; and I lay down my life for the sheep...For this reason the Father loves me, because I lay down my life, that I may take it again.

—John 10:14-15, 17

To the Holy Spirit, who filled my heart with love for my Creator.

To Gregory, my husband, who fought a courageous battle against cancer and lost, and to whom I promised I would indeed finish this book.

To all of God's creatures, both great and small, for bringing us closer to the face of God and encouraging us to sit upon the footstool of our Creator.

Contents

Part VII: A Call to Action

Acknowledgments

I offer thanks to God for my wonderful French-Canadian grandmother, Elizabeth Bennett Kinney, who took me to my first Catholic church when I was eight years old, thus lighting a fire in my soul that would not be quenched until I became a Catholic at age sixteen. I converted to Catholicism in 1966 and was instructed privately in the *Baltimore Catechism* by a dear monsignor in Miami, Florida, the Right Reverend Monsignor James F. Enright of Dublin, Ireland. He was, for me, the persona of Jesus, a wonderful priest who helped instill in me my fervor for the Catholic faith and my desire to study it more. What a journey it turned out to be, as my parents and sisters followed me a year later in their conversion to Catholicism.

I would also like to thank and acknowledge my ever-supportive and loving daughter, Seana, who brought me so much joy graduating college with her degree in theology, and who is my best friend! I would also like to thank her husband, David, my new son, who shares the Catholic faith with such joy!

I offer grateful thanks to the Roman Catholic Church, through which I have found the truths of the love and mercy of a great and good God, a Creator and Father, who wishes only that we love Him through Jesus so that we may love Him through eternity!

And finally, I would like to recognize the *Catechism of the Catholic Church*. The teachings of the one and perennial apostolic faith were extensively used in research for this book, in particular to underscore the truth that God is Creator of all, that which is seen and that which is unseen, both natural and supernatural, and that man has been called by his existence to glorify God in a mission of love and stewardship with his fellow man and the whole of creation.

Prologue

The Sting of Death

o o o o o o o o o o o o o o o o o o o o o o o o o o o o o o o o o o o o o
Trust in God! As we surrender what we love, we are cast into the bittersweet moment where we acknowledge God's divine providence for our beloved animal companions, and we walk in faith.

—Susi Pittman

"No, Rebel, you can't die! It's not fair, Mom, why does he have to die? Why can't the doctor save him? Please tell me he will be all right, please! I can't let him go ... please, no!"

My mother replied, "We can't help him now. He has to go home to God."

My beautiful white German shepherd, Rebel, had distemper. I later learned that distemper was a dreaded fatal virus for an unvaccinated young dog, causing a host of horrific symptoms and resulting in an agony-filled death if the animal is not euthanized. The man my father had bought Rebel from just over a year ago had given us forged papers on Rebel's inoculations, and now this beautiful creature was going to have to be put down.

I was devastated. I was twelve years old, and my world was coming to an end.

Rebel had been especially attached to me from the beginning—much to the dismay of my father, who had always held the top spot in the family dog's affection. But Rebel had chosen me to love the most, and I knew it. That made our relationship even more special! I was his and he was mine. It was like we had always known each other. We did everything together, energized by each other's presence. At night, he lay beside me on the bed, both of us in the blissful peace of God's care.

Rebel was my hero, my friend, my personal confidant. We were invincible together, and the world was ours to explore and share. Even today, I think of him and how connected we were; how we never spoke, yet understood one another perfectly; how we needed only to be close to each other.

It came to an abrupt end when one morning he could not get up. His hind legs dragged on the ground like dead weight. Yet his eyes were still aglow with joy, and his tongue hung from what I always called his "smiling face." It was so confusing. He was the same; his body was not.

The time to part came all too soon. I wasn't allowed to go with Rebel to the vet's office; I had to say good-bye to him at the house. I hugged his neck and stroked his back, cuddling his paw and crying so hard. He looked at me with such love and such sadness. I know he knew he was leaving, but everything about him said he was okay with that.

He was the first animal to show me acceptance of impending death—something I would witness time and again not only in my own pets, but also in wild animals. Rebel knew that he was going to die, but he also felt the Creator's call inside himself. And though I was only twelve, I saw and felt this very powerfully. I felt God in that moment—a moment that set me on a path with creation, though I could hardly know then what was to come.

As a hart longs for flowing streams, so longs my soul for thee, O God. My soul thirsts for God, for the living God. When shall I come and behold the face of God? My tears have been my food day and night, while men say to me continually, "Where is your God?"

(Psalm 42:1–3)

Introduction

o o o o o o o o o o o o o o o o o o o o o o o o o o o o o o o o o o o o

God our Father, may we love You in all things and above all things. Amen.

It is always hard to say good-bye. As Catholics, we know that our human loved ones are called by Christ to join Him in eternity, dwelling in heavenly bliss before God, enlightened by the light of glory, sharing in the fullness of the eternal life He has prepared for us.

But what about our pets, and the animals that fill the earth and our lives with such special beauty? Does God have a place for them? Where do animals go when they die? Are they just dust? Does God really care about any created beings besides man? Would God, who is Author of humankind and all creation, cast the nonhuman creation He called *good* into dust?

All of us who have loved at least one animal, or shared life with just one pet, have asked these questions.

Over the years I have searched the Church's teachings on the destiny of animals—though I've been interrupted by life at times during my quest. It was in the day-to-day sharing in creation that my young mind and heart were set free to love all that the natural world held. I found sanctuary on horseback, resting quietly amid granddaddy oaks covered in Spanish moss, my nose filled with the smell of Florida orange blossoms. God's voice in nature was powerful!

Yet the basic questions—how did it all come to be? Who was God? Why did He make me and all that I saw? What did God expect of me? Did He love me and the animals too?—continued to burn in my heart.

I knew that the beauty of nature and of natural creatures, by their very presence, spoke of God's goodness. It was something I didn't have to learn—I just knew. Something in them echoed a deep and abiding truth of the presence and concern of a loving Creator. It was the first and purest way that I came to love God, though I did not fully understand who God was, and I was a long way from knowing Him as Father. Those early years launched me on a lifetime journey to grow closer to Him, if only because I desired to know more about the One who created all that which I loved so much.

My husband, who was always my biggest cheerleader, had his own awakening to the beauty of natural creatures. As a young boy, he remembered shooting a beautiful red cardinal with a BB gun and killing it. When he went to pick up the little bird's lifeless body, it changed him forever. He wandered off with the bird in his hand and tears in his eyes, and he buried it. He never again had the desire to hurt other creatures!

As our life together over the years grew in joy and appreciation for created things, we found a growing commitment to abandoned animals—never turning any one of them away, we embraced them as new family members.

Eight nights before he died, Greg and I had a long talk. He said to me, "Susi, you gotta do your book! God needs you now, not in the same way He needs me, but He needs you to bring comfort to souls about their pets. You need to bring them the truth that we share in our faith."

It was his desire that I complete this work that was near and dear to both our hearts.

Following Greg's death, I took a pilgrimage of sorts. Not the usual religious pilgrimage to sacred ground—the type of journey that, as a couple, we loved to take—but a pilgrimage into nature, to be alone in creation. I was reminded of a scripture that I credit with great advice at that moment:

And he said to them, "Come away by yourselves to a lonely place, and rest a while." (Mark 6:31)

My destination was Cashiers, North Carolina, and my travel companion was the ever-exuberant Buddy, our three-year-old male Dalmatian. It was there, in a beautifully set rental cabin tucked back in the mountains—with a bear as my closest neighbor—that I found harmony with creation the way it was intended. The glory of God echoed in the surrounding nature like thunder! I had my morning coffee in the company of squirrels, and said my evening prayers in the presence of a shy brown bunny. Here I set this book's beginnings.

I write this book as a way of bringing peace to animal lovers who long to know the truth: that all creation was given its order, time, place, and purpose from its Creator, who sustains and preserves it at all times! All that God has created was produced in its proper nature and given its particular distinction. He is a God of purpose and promise, a Covenant-Maker who always delivers. As a Catholic layman, I have found great joy and peace in a merciful God who provides for all of His creation, keeping all in the palm of His Hand.

Thou sparest all things, for they are thine, O Lord who lovest the living. For thy immortal spirit is in all things. (Ws 11:26, 12:1)

The creatures that fill our lives are in the providential care of their God and in their appointed place. He does not forget a single existing life, since He is aware at all times of all that He has created. All of creation is ordered by God, coming forth from goodness and sharing in that goodness! Each creature is uniquely created, one from another, with endless variety in appearances, personalities, and habits, and each has its own individuality or personality given to it by God.

Jesus, the Son of God, was the *first*born of *all* creation. It pleased God to have all His fullness dwell within Jesus, His Son, through whom all creation would then enter the world. As the salvation story came to a climax, it was through Jesus, by the blood of the cross, that all of creation would be reconciled to God. Throughout the life of Jesus, animals were called to be witnesses to monumental moments. Farm animals kept watch at His birth; the donkey carried the Holy Family into exile in Egypt; wild animals were with Jesus when He spent forty days in the desert and was ministered to by angels; and a donkey carried Him again into Jerusalem preceding his death—a donkey that was prepared for Him by His own words. Why are the animals not only mentioned, but even participate as witnesses to their Lord's life?

God's ways are not our ways. There are many things that will forever remain a mystery until the human soul is again reunited with its Creator. We must be willing to accept these mysteries without ever losing hope in the goodness and perfect love that God has for all of creation—the perfect love offered through His Son, Jesus, for both humans and nonhumans. God's love and providential care are from age to age, forever, for all peoples.

Throughout this book, there are holy insights, sacred scriptures, traditions, and divine revelations for a better understanding of the Church's beautiful teachings on humankind and created things. Whether or not one believes that animals go to heaven does not hinder the salvation of one's soul. It is incidental to faith and the truth of salvation given to humankind in the Gospels. Yet it is a universal concern for stewards of creation who, in their humanness, consider such questions in their hearts. God has given humanity intellect to help us understand what God Himself says to us in creation by its presence, its reflective love of the Creator. As a child of God, you are endowed by Him with the ability to recognize His divine (*divinus*) providence (*provideo*) in all things. Providence, is God Himself considered in that act by which in His wisdom He so orders all events within the universe that the end for which it was created may be realized.[2] Creation comes forth from God's goodness and shares in that very same goodness.

More than just an answer to the destiny of our animal companions, this book is a journey closer to the God who loves and cares for all He has created.

This book specifically is not one person's fairytale or opinion about animal heaven. It examines the tenets of the Catholic faith on the subject of life beyond this world for animals and why Catholics may or may not believe in such. It encompasses God's creation of all things; the universal call to all humankind to be stewards of the earth; humanity's fall into disobedience and sin; the truth that Jesus came to redeem us and all of creation; and a look at this good and great God of covenants.

Chapters 25 through 27 are devoted to preparing your animal companion to pass and coping with the ensuing grief, offering support and help to those who are faced with or have faced saying good-bye to a pet member of the family. Over the years, I have lost many pets and nursed injured wild animals that died. To stand by one of our lesser brethren and ask that God receive back what is His is *never* easy. It is gut-wrenching and solemn. It is from experience that I write this section of the book, in hopes of sharing the walk with you in some way.

A call to action for all Catholics is found in chapter 28, "Catholic Stewards of Creation." A renewed spirit in responsible and informed Catholic stewardship of creation must be ignited as the world faces today's ecological, environmental, and climactic problems; animal issues; and the cosmic issues of the universe we live in. Chapter 28 will direct you to a new and exciting "rally point" to start your stewardship journey!

Start now your journey into faith. Faith takes all who search for the truth in the name of Jesus into the heart of redemption that God the Creator has prepared for the world.

If you seek a loving and just God, and you wish to understand His covenants with humankind and creation, you will find that the Creator has and always will have all creation perfectly planned and provided for!

"Ask, and it will be given you; seek, and you will find; knock, and it will be opened to you."
—Matthew 7:7

Part I
The Truth Is Out There

1

Why We Think Animals May Go to Heaven

o o o o o o o o o o o o o o o o o o o o o o o o o o o o o o o o o o o o
Heaven goes by favor. If it went by merit, you would stay out and your dog would go in.

—Mark Twain[3]

Mark Twain got it right: if we were not saved by grace, heaven would probably be going to the dogs! Pet lovers, at one time or another, have seen the beauty of God in their pets' eyes. Our pets, like creation, mirror God's love for us. So to tell animal lovers that their pets will be as dust into oblivion, and that their beloved animals hold no value or dignity before God, is like saying that God did not value the good He brought forth—and therefore He is a liar!

Of course, as Catholics, we know that God is not a liar, and that He is a God with a high tolerance for our misbehavior, prodigal tendencies, hearing-impaired willfulness, and general covenant-breaking. We have been nothing but trouble from day six—the day the Lord created us! Even with all of our incriminating credentials and loathsome disrespect, God sees His image in us and has held true to His covenant with humankind since the Garden of Eden. Thomas Aquinas acknowledged that God intended to communicate His perfection—His goodness—in the world.[4]

We surmise certain truths as we look at why we believe in heaven and a hereafter:

- There is but *one* God.
- Everything that God—who is perfect love—has created is good.

- All things were created to glorify God and return to Him.
- Man was given the unique ability to choose to love God in return.
- All other creation was given a *particular good.*
- God wants humankind and creation to join Him in perfection.
- God always existed; everything else that exists comes from God.
- God's love for us supersedes all boundaries and is beyond our power of understanding.
- God knows everything; He is the author of all, and that never changes.
- God has known intimately all that He has brought into existence. A trillion years from now, God will remember the first atom that He ever created for this universe.
- God lives outside of time in the "forever now," or eternity.
- In heaven, the thoughts and presence of God will never be absent from His creations. Human minds and bodies will sense the sights, sounds, and the wondrous beauty that most certainly will surround us.

What could be more beautiful than what God has prepared for the faithful? Referring to Isaiah 64:4, Saint Paul writes:

> But, as it is written, "What no eye has seen, nor ear heard, nor the heart of man conceived, what God has prepared for those who love him." (1 Cor. 2:9).

God gives us not only beautiful, created things, but also His only Son, Jesus, as a ransom for man and all of creation, our mediator between heaven and earth.

On this earth, all creation is evolving, according to the supernatural plan of God, toward a complete and perfect union with Him. In the magnificent book, *Crossing the Threshold of Hope*, Pope John Paul II alluded to the love that God the Father has for the world [5] by referencing the scripture, John 3:16:

> For God so loved the world that he gave his only Son, that whoever believes in him should not perish but have eternal life.

The world and man were consecrated through the power of the redemption.

All of this is a good foundation that leads us to feel that the all-powerful Creator has plans for everything created, both here and eternally, especially for those who love the Lord.

But then, there are also those incredible animal stories!

There are animals that save human beings; animals that manifest extraordinary courage; animals that exhibit an uncanny ability to show emotion, and even to cry; animals that can communicate, some with hierarchical methods and some with sign language; animals that know when a tornado or an earthquake is coming; animals that can smell cancer, drugs, termites (I use a termite service for my home that has such a dog, a beagle), and even the approach of an epileptic seizure; and animals that are transformed by the love of just one human being.

I recently read that various animal hospitals, zoos, and livestock houses are seeing success with the healing power of music from a harp.[6] Animals that exhibit anxiety or stress are allowed to listen to a CD of harp music. Their heart rates drop, respiration becomes more normal, and in some cases, the animals just doze off. Isn't it amazing that an instrument we humans consider heavenly in its sound would also induce such peaceful effects in animals! In some ways, we are not so far apart.

There are dog whisperers and horse whisperers who are a breed apart, so to speak, when it comes to communicating with certain types of animals. These humans have come to know their animal subjects through hours of observation, watching the subtle posturing, socialization activities, and body language of a species. These whisperers emanate a spirit of sincere goodwill and authority, peppered with honest affection that the animals truly sense and respond to! These gifted men and women have a God-given talent to connect with animals at the animals' communicative level. I'm not talking about psychic abilities; I am talking about people who understand the natural law and animal behavior at a higher level than do most other human beings. They tap into the secret language of an animal and are able to reach the most distant or troubled subjects.

What about all of that?

When I was younger, I read a book that came to symbolize everything I had always felt—and, in time, learned—about dogs and most of nature. W. Phillip Keller's *Lessons from a Sheepdog*,[7] speaks volumes about what a man, as a good steward, can do with a creature that despises human beings. Keller's journey in mending the untrusting heart of a dog and transforming both the dog and himself into new and beautiful creations is a lesson in divine salvation. Through subtle attempts to reach this beautiful dog, Lass, Keller comes to gain the dog's trust, and Lass places her life and her affections in her master's hands. In the patient process of reaching Lass, Keller sees the parallel between what he is doing with the dog and what God waits for and wants from us. It is a story for any animal lover who wants to know the secret of loving an animal well through the role that God intended for us, and it helps illustrate the truth of a loving God who providentially cares for all He has created.

There is also the horse whisperer, Monty Roberts. His observational skills and listening ability with horses is world-renowned. He broke the secret language of *Equus*, communicating with horses by reading their body language and sending similar signals back. He never *broke* a horse with the abusive practices. He conducted what he called *gentling*. Now there's a great term for you! This gifted man not only had communicative talents with horses, but also with deer, jokingly referring to himself as "multilingual."[8]

Many Catholics may not know that Pope Benedict XVI has been a cat lover for a long time. In his boyhood years, the Holy Father had a great affinity for nature and animals, and he received pets as Christmas gifts. In his adult years, he always had a cat or cats about him; his brother, Father Georg Ratzinger, cares for the family cats today. When the Holy Father was Cardinal Ratzinger, his care for the stray cats that lived about the Vatican area was renowned in Rome. He nursed the injured and sick ones, feeding many of the cats that took up residence close to where he lived. There was a time when so many cats followed him to the Vatican that a Swiss Guard was heard to remark that he thought the cats were "laying siege to the Holy See."[9]

There has been much published in recent years regarding near-death experiences (NDEs). These are out-of-body experiences of adults and children who are said to be clinically dead. Their souls leave their bodies, traveling either into the light or into total darkness. These people see what is happening to their bodies from above—in some cases at great distance—and are later able to describe in detail what was happening around them.[10] NDEs occur in all cultures and in all faiths. The study of NDEs has gone mainstream, and many doctors, psychologists, and scientists are involved in frontline research into this awakening field. The research shows that there are basically two groups: no matter what the religious background or personal beliefs of the subjects, there are those who have a *good* experience and those who have a *bad* experience.[11]

Those experiencing the good almost always describe entering some type of light, tunnel, cosmic radiance, or glowing emanation. This is accompanied with feelings of peace and joy, a sensation of time speeding up, a heightened sense of awareness, and a sense of crossing into another world. They meet family or friends who have died; experience completeness, a total peace, and embracing love; and have a sense of the presence of a divine personage. There also is a sense of leaving a place of exile (earth) and returning home—something not sensed while present in the human body.[12]

Adults and children alike have described seeing family pets, petting and embracing pets, and even seeing other animals and created things, such as flowers, trees, birds, and mountains. They hear incredible music and see colors that our human eyes could not bear to see because of the brilliance and diffusive nature of the glorified natural. I find it especially poignant that young children see such things, as they have no preconceived ideas to interfere with the experience.[13]

Only in the recounting of those who have experienced the good do we find what would be defined as a heavenly experience, in which animals and creation are seen in a new luminosity.

It is very comforting and hopeful to hear such accounts. Those experiencing the good have no fear of death upon their return to their bodies, and most come back with a sense of mission.[14]

Those who have bad NDEs describe being cast into darkness—a sense of falling through dark space and taken into nothingness. They describe themselves as feeling anxious, hopeless, and fearful, surrounded by an unseen—yet palpably evil and menacing—presence or force. Never once has anyone who had a bad NDE recounted seeing any earthly animals during the experience, which most all considered to be a visit to hell. Bad NDEs have included descriptions of other-worldly or demonic creatures present in a pervading darkness over a barren terrain or turbulent flames in a shining darkness. The bad NDE group showed a significant change toward better behavior and a more value-oriented life upon returning to their bodies.[15]

As Catholics, we certainly believe what Jesus has told us: that humanity, given free will and intellect, will either choose to be with Him eternally in heaven, or with Satan eternally in damnation.

People who experience good NDEs perceive that they are in heaven and see animals and creation; those who experience bad NDEs recount nothing of animals.[16] The study of NDEs certainly lends credence to the doctrinal truth that Jesus is connected to all material creation that is *good*. Heavenly views of human and nonhuman creation, glorified, would be indicative of Jesus's redeeming power over all things.

Catholic saints and visionaries down through the ages have been given insight and knowledge regarding heaven. One great Catholic saint that comes to mind is Saint John Bosco, also called Don Bosco. God allowed Don Bosco to see the part of heaven that was explained by Don Bosco's guide as being the "glorified natural," a place where creation appeared in its glorified state.[17]

Veterinarians have their own stories of animal miracles that occur in their offices: wonderful, heartwarming stories that involve saving a pet from the fringe of death; lost animals that overcome tremendous odds to be reunited with their families; animals that express joy of being or spirit; animals that communicate almost telepathically with their caregivers; material signs following the death of a pet, either witnessed or felt, of something beyond this world. You can watch just one episode of any animal-rescue program or emergency-vet program on television and know that something more powerful than medicine is at work there. The eyes of the animals as they are held with loving arms show surrender to and unconditional trust in the humans caring for their needs.

The saints who have received private revelations from Mary, Mother of Jesus, tell us that on occasion, the Blessed Mother is seen with a bird or birds about her. It is remarkable to note that at the Blessed Mother's home in Ephesus, Turkey, which was built for her and in which she lived with St. John the Beloved, birds abound. The area is known as *Bulbul Dag,* which means "Mountain of Nightingales."[18]

All these examples of the tremendous presence and power of animals in our lives lead us to consider that surely these creatures would be provided for in heaven by a loving God.

Bonds between humans and animals are as powerful as those between father and son or mother and daughter. To deny this or want to ignore it does not allow for God's healing hand to help man toil with God for the good of all He has created. Take a look at what Wisdom 13:5 says:

For from the greatness and beauty of created things comes a corresponding perception of their Creator.

We must remember, though, that animals are what they are. They are not human. All animals were created according to God's own unique design and are hardwired differently in their relationship with the Creator than is humankind, requiring the same yet different providential care as God gives to humanity. Animals live among us with usual, unusual, and even inspiring behaviors that suggest an undercurrent of some unseen power that sustains and dignifies their existence. God has considerations for all creation! Take heart!

There is much in sacred scripture that gives us hope to believe in the providential care of creation by God, both here and renewed. Isn't that the crux of our existence, that we always hope in the Lord? Should we not embrace what He Himself in the Second Person has embraced by becoming human and material? Jesus embraced all of creation, not just man. He knows how very much we love, and what and whom we love!

No animal can be more important than a human soul, nor should we obsess unnecessarily over our lesser brethren in the animal world. But animals are a gift, and we should respect them and all creation with the dignity and value given them by God. God has given of Himself to all that is nonhuman to receive to the degree that He can fill it. Nonhumans maintain a unique relationship with God, as does the human part of creation.

From the book of Isaiah comes a descriptive metaphor of the coming of Jesus into the world:

The wolf shall dwell with the lamb, and the leopard shall lie down with the kid, and the calf and the lion and the fatling together, and a little child shall lead them. The cow and the bear shall feed; their young shall lie down together; and the lion shall eat straw like the ox. The sucking child shall play over the hole of the asp, and the weaned child shall put his hand on the adder's den. They shall not hurt or destroy in all my holy mountain; for the earth shall be full of the knowledge of the Lord as the waters cover the sea. (Isa. 11:6–9)

This glorious description by Isaiah is very poignant in its use of animals to create this vision of peaceful harmony. Why didn't Isaiah use more humanistic terms? Was he just poetic that day and wanted his words to be flowery? Or perhaps he chose to describe the scene in this way because creation is God's loving reflection, offering a glimpse of both God's face and His desire for all things on earth to be brought into renewal with the coming messianic times.

It certainly gives us hope in the coming of a new heaven and a new earth as proclaimed in Revelation, where we find another verse of encouragement:

And I heard every creature in heaven and on earth and under the earth and in the sea, and all therein, saying, "To him who sits upon the throne and to the Lamb be blessing and honor and glory and might for ever and ever!" (Rev. 5:13)

Sacred scripture is very clear that every living thing will praise the return of Jesus the Christ as He is Redeemer of all and lifts all that He has created into His eternal hands.

"All that the Father gives me will come to me."

(John 6:37)

2

Why We Think Animals May Not Go to Heaven

o o o o o o o o o o o o o o o o o o o o o o o o o o o o o o o o o o o o o

In Christianity neither morality nor religion come into contact with reality at any point.

—Friedrich Nietzsche[19]

Thank you, Friedrich; you are a good place to start. Friedrich Nietzsche was an existentialist—a person who believes that human beings are basically responsible for creating their own meaning in life. He was also an atheist, believing that God does not exist. Nietzsche was one of the fathers of radical individualism. His vision can be summarized thusly: all things are relative; science is one's religion; a God or a divine creative force in the universe that orchestrated all things is improbable. As a matter of fact, he pronounced God "dead" and said that Christianity was the faith of little men; all things pass into nothingness; there are no spiritual realities.[20]

Next, let us consider the agnostics. They believe that it is impossible to know whether God does or does not exist because the human mind cannot reach that far. Well, hey, that may apply to my brother Earl, but some of us *can* reach that far! (Only kidding. I don't have a brother Earl, and I do believe that each soul is stamped by God with a knowing that God exists.)

Then there are the lukewarm Christians who are not committed to Jesus in any particular way—just only when it suits them. They are uncommitted and self-indulgent, with a "what-serves-me-best" philosophy perpetuated in personal justification in this world. Most in this category don't believe in hell, and just hope that maybe heaven exists. This is dangerous ground for true believers, for it is here that we can become the devil's fodder! One of the most important references that I recall from my studies into Satanism and the occult, which aptly conveys this concept, states: "Do what thou wilt shall be the whole of the law."[21]

Many who fall into one of these three categories—along with a surprising number of Christians—feel that their pets or animals have no other existence but to serve man. They believe that God intended animals to be only brute, stupid beasts, designed to satisfy man's needs while on earth in whatever way man chooses to use them without need of dignity or humane treatment. Those who believe this treat animals as chattel or property, something they can keep or throw away at their discretion. Our humane societies, animal-control centers, and animal-rescue organizations are full of animals that have been tossed away. Yet these animals are the lucky ones. They weren't just dropped off somewhere on a side street or in the deep woods to fend for themselves, facing starvation and/or certain death if not found by a charitable soul.

Christians of all cultures also use animals for blood sports. Don't even think of telling those who enjoy these self-centered, guts-and-glory displays that it isn't the right thing to do. They'll give you every justification in the world! I can certainly understand hunting when it serves a cultural group, such as an indigenous people who must hunt to feed or clothe themselves. But I don't see trophy hunting in the forest or on the high seas as a noble calling— especially when the hunters are armed with high-tech killing or catching equipment that gives man license to slaughter in the name of sport. The false honor given the poor bulls slaughtered in the bullfighting ring is a cruel abomination. The dog-fighting and cock-fighting rings are simply displays of blood lust from hateful people. Those in the horse-breeding and horse-racing industries certainly turn a blind eye to the thousands of horses that are rejected and discarded like so much refuse, only to be sent to the slaughterhouses to end up as dog food or steaks for human consumption. The commercial fishing industry fares no better, though work has been done among American fishers to protect certain species of mammals, cetaceans, and sea turtles from entrapment.

All of these practices are supported by the notion that animals do not exist beyond this world. After all, it is much easier to treat animals poorly if they are viewed only as disposable earthly chattel.

In addition, some of our Catholic clergy are quick to discount heaven for animals. It is confusing, to say the least, when Catholic priests from around the world don't always match up in their theology. The faithful are told—sometimes tragically—that "we don't believe in that!" or "that subject is absolutely trivial." This attitude shows total disregard for those caring and concerned souls who answer the creation stewardship calling from God. It takes the importance of God's plan for the ultimate perfecting of all creation and tosses it aside!

Lastly, there is the "cosmic consciousness" that holds that all things meld together, recirculating and reticulating and reincarnating into some type of perfected continuity, where God is evil in His ultimate nature and man is divine in his true nature. The popularity of "New Age" philosophies has certainly heightened this belief, and it continues to attract followers from all walks of life. In the Church document titled *Jesus Christ, the Bearer of the Water of Life*,[22] the dangers of New Age thinking are outlined. No matter the nuances, New Age practices and beliefs are occult in nature and in no way support a Catholic way of life.

I believe that humans are born with the knowledge of God. John Scotus believed that scripture was given to man by God to help him remember what was placed on his heart at his creation and that sin had made him forget.[23]

God Himself states the truth about our beginnings to the prophet Jeremiah:

"Before I formed you in the womb I knew you, and before you were born I consecrated you." (Jer. 1:5)

My question is: Can anyone show me where God says that humans are the *only* creation of value that matters as absolute truth? Humanity is uniquely united to the Creator with a soul, yes, but we are also part of the bigger family of creation in general, and creation is also given value by its Creator. Is it so hard to understand that animals created by God with a *particular good* would not also have knowledge of their Creator?

As much as hope in a continuance for animal companions can be called into question, it is no less questionable than believing that nonhuman creatures have no value, dignity, or right of continuance before their Creator.

Suffice it to say that the "no" and "not" type answers given by some clergy on the destiny of animals are insensitive. Such answers can mislead the ministerial intentions of the faithful who care for creation away from a deeper relationship with Jesus and away from the work God has asked of them. If man isn't at peace with God, he isn't at peace with His creation.

3

The Church on Creation

o o o o o o o o o o o o o o o o o o o o o o o o o o o o o o o o o o o o
For the Lord has made all things, and to the godly he has granted wisdom.

—Sirach 43:33

I have heard friends and fellow parishioners voice their dismay that they don't know what the Church says about the destiny of other creatures of creation, especially the companion animals we call our pets.

I have thought, "Been there, and I know what you mean!"

I believe those who feel so unsure or lost on this question are not alone. It isn't a subject that is exactly trumpeted from the "ambo" or pulpit into the pews.

The Catholic Church cannot tell you whether or not your Uncle Charlie is in purgatory or Hitler is in hell or your beloved pet is in heaven, any more than it can tell you what day the world is going to end. The Church can say with authority who is a saint in heaven. The Church also speaks with authority to us on the final climax in the redemption story as all things in heaven and on earth are called by Jesus into renewal!

Eternal providence for creation is a powerful and emotional subject that evokes definitive personal beliefs. We all have them. I certainly do! But there is one thing I know, and that is that the Church will never lead me into error and seeks only to save my soul from hell.

A quick look at history shows that the Roman Catholic Church began with Jesus Christ, who commanded the apostles, including Peter, the first pope of the Church, to preach the gospel. This is the most important mission, set forth from the beginning through the apostles: the salvation of human souls. The apostles entrusted the sacred tradition and sacred scripture to the Church.

The Old and New Testaments comprise the Bible. The early written Bible was comprised of different sections in three different languages—Hebrew, Aramaic, and Greek—and was first translated into Latin in the second century.[24] Today the Catholic Church contains the complete, authentic, and true Bible, and Catholics can share a great sense of heritage and connection to their ancient Judeo-Christian roots! The Church brings us to salvation in Jesus, which is another reason I write this book.

What the Church *can* tell you, with authority, is found in the Bible and brought to the catechism of the Catholic Church, where this question is posed:

Where does everything that exists come from and where is it going?[25]

And the answer:

He who chose the patriarchs, who brought Israel out of Egypt, and who by choosing Israel created and formed it, this same God reveals himself as the One to whom belong all the peoples of the earth, and the whole of earth itself; he is the One who alone "made heaven and earth."[26]

The universe was created "in a state of journeying" (in statu viae) toward an ultimate perfection yet to be attained, to which God has destined it.[27]

God in His divine providence, His care, and His eternal foresight of all things guides all creation to its perfect end. It is the knowledge that all things are seen by God and asked to abide with God; that animals, by their infused essence of having been created, are good; and that humankind, in our intellect, allows God's will to lead us.

But what is this destiny that finally is adjudicated to creation? And when does it occur?

We know that humanity receives a "particular judgment" upon death, but what about the rest of creation—the nonhuman part? Are animals held in reserve, or do they pass quickly into the hands of God?

The Church cannot answer these questions with any authority, as these matters remain a mystery known only to God, so we are referred to the catechism, which comments on the book of Revelation regarding the end of time:

> Sacred Scripture calls this mysterious renewal, which will transform humanity and the world, "new heavens and a new earth." It will be the definitive realization of God's plan to bring under a single head "all things in Christ], things in heaven and things on earth."[28] ...
>
> The visible universe, then, is itself destined to be transformed, "so that the world itself, restored to its original state, facing no further obstacles, should be at the service of the just," sharing their glorification in the risen Jesus Christ.[29]
>
> *"We know neither the moment of the consummation* of the earth and of man, nor the way in which the universe will be transformed."[30]

At the appointed time, the material world—which includes animals, all created things, and the universe—will attain its destiny with humanity and will be brought to perfection through Jesus Christ. Does that mean that only the animals that are alive at the time of this renewal will be transformed? Or are our animal friends that have died or are dying today provided for too?

All creation "rests" in Jesus and waits to be brought to fulfillment by Him. All things will be united in Christ, and each will be transformed—given its perfected destiny with God whether at the end of time, or sooner.

The mind and providence of God is infinite. When we think that what was and is and will be cannot be retained and eternally provided for, then we are putting limits on the unlimited power of God. God's love supersedes death for all that He has created! I can remember when I was growing up, sometimes there would be really hard things to deal with in life, and my father would always say to me, "Nothing is impossible with God." The fulfillment of God's divine providence in this world is no less impossible.

I hold great hope in seeing once again all those creatures that I have cared for in this life. Will I see my beloved animals upon my death, or at the end of time? I don't worry about how or if that might happen. Our Creator has promised His divine providence to all that He has created! What an awesome promise to rest your doubts upon!

I believe there are many animal lovers who feel that an animal passes to God in an immediate way; but it is not a belief shared by all. Does this make it right or wrong? No. It is one of those mysteries that we will simply have to endure until we stand face-to-face with God.

I have had personal experiences at the death of some of my animals that speak of the miraculous, but I hold those privately and adhere to what the Church teaches me to be truth. Those experiences have enhanced my love for and belief in God, and have certainly spurred me on to serve as a better steward of creation. Were these experiences necessary for my salvation? No. But they have inspired me to love God more and believe in His promises.

Saint Francis of Assisi valued the earth and its creation as God's home, looking at himself as a steward of God's holy ground. We could all learn from his example.

The Catholic Church includes creation in the sacramental life of the Church. The water and olive oil are brought to be blessed by consecrated hands and made holy for the seven sacraments: baptism, confirmation, Eucharist, penance, holy orders, matrimony, and anointing of the sick. The bread and wine are brought to the altar of the Lord for transubstantiation, giving to us the body and blood, soul and divinity, of Jesus Christ as spiritual food:

> So Jesus said to them, "Truly, truly, I say to you, unless you eat the flesh of the Son of man and drink his blood, you have no life in you; he who eats my flesh and drinks my blood has eternal life, and I will raise him up at the last day. As the living Father sent me, and I live because of the Father, so he who eats me will live because of me. This is the bread which came down from heaven, not such as the fathers ate and died; he who eats this bread will live for ever." This he said in the synagogue as he taught at Capernaum. (John 6:53–54, 57–59)

Take time at your next Mass to give reverence to and thanks for God's transforming power over creation, especially in the reception of the Holy Eucharist.

Catholics celebrate the Holy Sacrifice of the Mass, and the Church reaffirms in the liturgy that the whole family of creation shares in the worship of its Creator:[31] It would, therefore, seem appropriate that each weekend as we attend Mass, we notice the creation about us—in our yards, on the drive to church, on the way home—and offer a prayer of thanksgiving to the loving God who created it all for us.

God has told us throughout the scriptures that He indeed is the end in which all created things reside—an eternal existence that remains a mystery for now, as we do not know exactly how that will come about.

Heaven, which is the destination for all that God loves, is a real place, with unimagined glories especially for us. The truth is that God will not keep from us a single thing that would contribute to our happiness with Him. Our hope always rests in the Lord who made us, who knows our deepest feelings and desires, and especially how greatly we have loved and been loved in our lives.

> We firmly believe that God is master of the world and of its history. But the ways of his providence are often unknown to us. Only at the end, when our partial knowledge ceases, when we see God "face to face," will we fully know the ways by which—even through the dramas of evil and sin—God has guided his creation to that definitive sabbath rest for which he created heaven and earth.[32]

The intellectuals of today, like the ancient Greeks, propagate pragmatic philosophies regarding man's getting into heaven. Jesus made the entry requirements pretty clear:

> "Truly, I say to you, whoever does not receive the kingdom of God like a child shall not enter it." (Mark 10:15)

To be "like a child" means to be completely trusting. In your trust, you are obedient in all things to the One you trust. You trust the One in whom your faith lies to bring about perfect happiness for you in perfect good, and to guide you in your life's journey; and you believe in the promises given.

Take a moment to think about how your pet lives its whole life trusting you for its well-being and sustenance, and you will touch upon the trust you, too, must have in your Creator and eternal provider. Trust the One who created you to prepare unending joy that is uniquely yours.

Many writings by John Paul II touch my soul with musings of how very small our existence is here, on a miniscule orb in the vastness of space, as compared to the infinity of wondrous things awaiting those who love the Lord.

Right now, if we are rightly oriented in the Lord, we are all on a mission to fulfill God's supernatural plan as only we can. Part of that mission includes stewardship of creation. Animals and creation, animate and inanimate—all are created to glorify God and are ever subject to their Creator, who shares them with man.

Man's dominion over inanimate and other living beings granted by the Creator is not absolute.[33]

Animals are God's creatures. He surrounds them with his providential care. By their mere existence they bless him and give him glory.[34]

If you do not have the *Catechism of the Catholic Church* or *The Catholic Study Bible*,[35] please get one. Both are very, very easy to use. There is so much explained in great detail in the catechism that you are sure to find answers to many more questions besides "What are the Church's teachings on creation?" and "Is there a heaven for my pet?" And read your "wisdom books": Job, Psalms, Proverbs, Ecclesiastes, Song of Songs, Wisdom, and Sirach. These books include great moral and spiritual teachings as well as awesome truths!

Ultimately, the voice of God speaking in the treasure that is the Roman Catholic faith gives us cause to celebrate the redemption and renewal of all things through Jesus, Lord of all creation!

"For I have come down from heaven, not to do my own will, but the will of him who sent me; and this is the will of him who sent me, that I should lose nothing of all that he has given me, but raise it up at the last day."

(John 6:38–39)

4

Jesus, Lord of Creation

ooooooooooooooooooooooooooooooooooo

*He is the image of the invisible God, the first-born of all creation;
for in him all things were created, in heaven and on earth, visible
and invisible, whether thrones or dominions or principalities or
authorities—all things were created through him and for him. He
is before all things, and in him all things hold together. He is the
head of the body, the church; he is the beginning, the first-born
from the dead, that in everything he might be pre-eminent. For in
him all the fullness of God was pleased to dwell, and through him
to reconcile to himself all things, whether on earth or in heaven,
making peace by the blood of his cross.*

—Colossians 1:15–20

The union of the divine with the human material in the personage of
Jesus Christ—Word of God, Son of God, Second Person of the Holy
Trinity, Lord of Creation—is the foundation of all blessings upon man
and upon the whole of creation.

Jesus came to substitute His obedience to God for humankind's
disobedience to God, which began in the Garden of Eden. All of
creation was affected as Jesus brought renewal to all. All things
remain subject to His will at all times, even though He chose to
place into human hands the stewardship of all created things.
All things everywhere in the created universe are gift and grace,
and they ultimately obey Jesus's command. Jesus, who, by His
salvific action, renews the natural realm established by God.

And Jesus cried out and said, "He who believes in me, believes not in me but in him who sent me. And he who sees me sees him who sent me." (John 12:44–45)

Here Jesus reiterates for our benefit that He is indeed the Son of God, proceeding from the Father as perfect self-expression and meriting His Lordship over all that exists.

We find in the book of John that Jesus, who is the Word, was always with God, and it was through Jesus that all things were made.

In the beginning was the Word, and the Word was with God, and the Word was God. He was in the beginning with God; all things were made through him, and without him was not anything made that was made. (John 1:1–3)

Jesus, Lord of Creation, united Himself to our humanity, inviting us to receive His spirit of love, truth, simplicity, peace, obedience, and transformation, and to share it with the whole of creation.

Jesus, being divine, the second person of the Godhead, had supernatural capabilities that He used to do His Father's will at every moment of His life, bringing about the redemption of the world. Jesus approaches us from the Creator as the one through whom all things were created. He is given authority to redeem all things for the Creator as Peter says:

Simon Peter answered him, "Lord to whom shall we go? You have the words of eternal life; and we have believed, and have come to know that you are the Holy One of God." (John 6:68-69)

His divinity—though in human form, living among humanity—was clearly made manifest. We see in the following points that creation responds to His will throughout the New Testament:

• Jesus entered into His humanity through the womb of Mary. Mary conceived Jesus by divine impregnation as the Holy Spirit overshadowed her (Luke 1).
• Jesus was born of a virgin (Matt. 1 and Luke 1).

- During the wedding at Cana, Jesus changed water into wine (John 2).
- Jesus raised the dead numerous times, including the young man at Nain (Luke 7), the daughter of Jarius (Matt. 9, Mark 5, and Luke 8), and his friend Lazarus (John 11).
- Jesus fills Simon's fish nets with fish (Luke 5).
- Jesus cast out demons from possessed people (Matt. 8 and Mark 1 and 5).
- Jesus feeds the four thousand men and their families with seven loaves and a few fish (Matt. 15 and Mark 8).
- Jesus and the fish with a coin in its mouth to pay taxes (Matt. 17).
- Jesus healed the sick with words or with His touch (Matt. 8, 9, and 15; Mark 14; Luke 17; and John 9).
- Jesus restores a severed ear (Luke 22).
- Jesus quells the storm and calms the sea (Mark 4).

Only the Lord of Creation is capable of such feats. All natural and supernatural creation responds to the Lord; even the demons were neutralized by the authority of Jesus.

It is awesome and amazing to imagine that Jesus loves all, renews all, and invites us to share His inheritance with His Father, our Creator in heaven. We need only trust that Jesus is the Messiah.

Both animate and inanimate creation share in a communion of praises to God by their very presence, in their beauty, in their sounds, and as a reflection of God's love. All of creation is subject to change, made by the One who was, is, and will be "changeless" forever.

Jesus, the Beautiful One, Lord of Creation, has brought into this world nothing that He loathes. All was created for good through which the infinite goodness can radiate. Humankind, especially, has been called upon to find God in all creatures—much as Saint Francis of Assisi did—and to walk this world with them as brethren.

As much as we may wish to know everything possible, God intends some things to remain great mysteries that lead us to an internal call to faith. We lose so much when we feel we have to "dog-ear" the mysteries of life—dissecting, researching, and analyzing to death those things that are unseen gifts of divine providence.

Think about this for a moment: until humanity's free will is perfected, why would God entrust us with something so important as understanding a great mystery while the possibility of humanity's abuse of such a mystery still exists? Human common sense dictates that mysteries must exist, perhaps sometimes to save us from ourselves. A mystery demands faith to believe that some things God keeps, in His goodness, from us.

Our faith journey leads to the love and mercy that is God our Creator, who has reconciled man and creation with Himself through His Son, Jesus the Christ. Because of Jesus, all creation lives in providential hope for its ultimate destiny with its Creator.

Jesus deliberately with divine purpose chose to offer Himself up in sacrifice so that the Father's will for all creation would be fulfilled. Only by Jesus's death and resurrection are the chains of death broken for all things. Life begins anew, and the journey to the perfection that God intended comes to pass!

Jesus takes that which we ignore, abuse, and obliterate, and raises it up as He redeems all of creation. He and He alone was the perfect fit between heaven and earth, binding all together, sustaining all, and redeeming all to an ultimate perfection and unity.

Jesus Christ, having entered the sanctuary of heaven once and for all, intercedes constantly for us as the mediator who assures us of the permanent outpouring of the Holy Spirit.[36]

Part II
Recognizing God's Plan

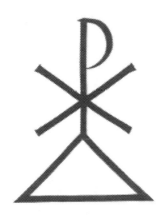

5

In the Beginning

○ ○
Creation is the foundation of "all God's saving plans," the "beginning of the history of salvation" that culminates in Christ.[37]

The revelation of creation was, in essence, the first covenant of God with His people. Understanding how the Creator assimilates all of creation, how He creates order among human and nonhuman, and how He accommodates each and every part, requires starting at the beginning of time. The first three chapters of Genesis give us the truths of creation, how it begins and ends in God.

- God always existed.
- He is the universal cause of all that exists.
- He has no beginning or end, being the Great "I Am Who Am," the eternal Alpha and Omega.

These truths about God cannot ever be fully understood in this lifetime, perhaps not even in eternity. God has no other reason to create anything except that He does it out of goodness and love, to share Himself as Creator with His creatures. The Bible records in sacred scripture these truths: that all was created by God, brought in to being through the Word, which is Jesus, by the power of God's love, and is sustained by God's breath, the Holy Spirit. All things live and have their being in a created world.

There are two distinct Creation scriptures or texts, one in the Old Testament and one in the New Testament. Both texts establish the beginning of the natural universe and introduce the Triune God: a Father/Creator, Son/Word, and Holy Spirit/Breath.

In the Old Testament, we read:

In the beginning God created the heavens and the earth. The earth was without form and void, and darkness was upon the face of the deep; and the Spirit of God was moving over the face of the waters. And God said, "Let there be light"; and there was light. And God saw that the light was good. (Gen. 1:1–4)

The New Testament says:

In the beginning was the Word, and the Word was with God, and the Word was God. He was in the beginning with God. (John 1:1–2)

In Genesis 1 is recorded the moment of universal creation. God creates everything and brings all out of nothingness into existence, calls it "good," and God reiterates how good it is six more times!

And God saw that it was good. (Gen. 1:10, 12, 18, 21, 25)

And God saw everything that he had made, and behold, it was very good. (Gen. 1:31).

Why do you think God felt it that important to repeat Himself to us? Because God wants us to know He is true *good*! But what is meant by "good"?

"Good" is the effect of the cause, which is love. Only pure good can flow from such a cause! If we don't understand anything else, God wants us to understand this. The universe and all in it was brought into being by the source of love Himself. It was so then; it is so now; and it will be so until the end of time. Love is the most powerful force in all that exists. All of creation is a reflection of that divine love. Everything that God has created in its singularity and uniqueness is a holy book, full of the Word of God. Isn't it great to know that we walk on and about sacred ground every day!

The *hierarchy of creatures* is expressed by the order of the "six days," from the less perfect to the more perfect. God loves all his creatures and takes care of each one, even the sparrow.[38]

Genesis records that God created the entire universe—the earth, all of the elements, minerals, rocks, plants, trees, and vegetation—in the first four days (though we know the length of God's days are not our days). All plant life is part of the living, a majestic gift of our Creator; it is the nonhuman part of creation that, along with the animated creatures, receives the providential care of the Father.

The reference to "day" and "night" shows that God was indeed ordering the cosmos and setting this beautiful blue planet into orbit around the sun in the vastness of the created universe.

The creation of animated creatures began on the fifth day, when God brought into being the creatures from the waters and seas and all the birds and winged creatures.

And God said, "Let the waters bring forth swarms of living creatures, and let birds fly above the earth across the firmament of the heavens. … Be fruitful and multiply and fill the waters in the seas, and let birds multiply on the earth." And there was evening and there was morning, a fifth day. (Gen. 1:20–23)

On the sixth day, God created the land creatures—those animals that would be walking with and among man—and He brings creation to a climax with the creation of man. Man is the crown of creation, positioned to carry forth for God the responsible and loving stewardship towards all created things. He is placed in the position of being a cooperator with God and His will.

And God said, "Let the earth bring forth living creatures according to their kinds: Cattle and creeping things and beasts of the earth according to their kinds." And it was so.

And God made the beasts of the earth according to their kinds and the cattle according to their kinds, and everything that creeps upon the ground according to its kind. And God saw that it was good.

Then God said, "Let us make man in our image, after our likeness; and let them have dominion over the fish of the sea, and over the birds of the air, and over the cattle, and over all the earth, and over every creeping thing that creeps upon the earth."

So God created man in his own image, in the image of God he created him ...

And God said, "Behold, I have given you every plant yielding seed which is upon the face of all the earth, and every tree with seed in its fruit; you shall have them for food.

And to every beast of the earth, and to every bird of the air, and to everything that creeps on the earth, everything that has the *breath of life*, I have given every green plant for food." And it was so.

And God saw everything that he had made, and behold it was very good. And there was evening and there was morning, a sixth day. (Gen. 1:24–27, 29–31)

The *breath of God* (Holy Spirit) is the "sustainer" of all life everywhere; the Spirit was given through the *light of God* (Jesus, the Word). Creation received life from the Holy Spirit according to its particular kind and in the diversity that God intended. The Spirit continues to act in all creation and has done so down through the ages. God created all that is in the world for man because God willed to do so.

God willed the diversity of his creatures and their own particular goodness, their interdependence, and their order. He destined all material creatures for the good of the human race. Man, and through him all creation, is destined for the glory of God.[39]

It is important to note that when God created the animals and man, both received the "breath of life" from God. Both are destined for the glory of God, each according to its kind.

"And to every beast of the earth, and to every bird of the air, and to everything that creeps on the earth, everything that has the breath of life, I have given every green plant for food." (Gen. 1:30)

Then the Lord God formed man of dust from the ground, and breathed into his nostrils the breath of life; and man became a living being. (Gen. 2:7)

Saint Francis always called the animals the "lesser brethren," recognizing the big difference between humans and the rest of the created world is the soul, the image of God that was given to us. The soul includes intellect or intelligence and free will:

Then God said, "Let us make man in our image, after our likeness." (Gen. 1:26)

Humankind being made in the image of God and having a soul does not make us equal to God. On the contrary, we will remain forever inferior to God who is our Creator. Compared to God, humankind is always as nothing. Yet God wishes only to draw His human creation closer to Himself, and wants us to choose to love Him back, so that we and God may share in perfect love eternally in Heaven. This is a covenant between God the Creator and humankind. God places us in a unique relationship with Him because humans are given eternal souls imaged after the likeness of God; this allows us to share in God's eternal love in a deeper way than other created things can.

It was God's desire that all things of heaven and earth proceed through the second person of the Trinity, the Word, the One who existed with God always, the One we would come to know as Jesus. Through the Word, all of creation was created for a specific purpose, and nothing was created randomly or accidentally.

And before him no creature is hidden, but all are open and laid bare to the eyes of him with whom we have to do. (Heb. 4:13)

All things have a place and time to reach their particular fulfillment or mission as ordained by God. The loving providence of a Father for all He has created and sustains in the universe is made manifest in the books of Wisdom and Sirach, which commemorate the Creator's promise that nothing is created in vain, and nothing is without meaning. Meaning is not created by us, but is given by God.

> For from the greatness and beauty of created things comes a corresponding perception of their Creator. (Ws 13:5)

> For the Most High knows all that may be known, and he looks into the signs of the age. He declares what has been and what is to be, and he reveals the tracks of hidden things. No thought escapes him, and not one word is hidden from him. He has ordained the splendors of his wisdom, and he is from everlasting and to everlasting. (Sir 42:18–21)

When we awake in the mornings, we properly should give thanks to God for seeing us through yet another night, and on to our mission—our meaning in life—and into the new day.

But how many of us do that?

Have you ever noticed how the birds are always first up in the morning giving their voices in praise and thanksgiving to their Creator for yet another day's existence? This is a lesson in humility for us, when we realize how the lesser brethren remember God, but we awake remembering a bad night's sleep or an aching back.

All of creation, no matter how small or seemingly insignificant, has meaning in, through, and with Christ through whom it was created. God's voice in creation requires no speech and crosses all boundaries of created things.[40]

> How greatly to be desired are all his works, and how sparkling they are to see! All these things live and remain forever for every need, and are all obedient. (Sir 42:22–23)

In summary:

- God always existed.
- He is the universal cause of all that exists.
- He has no beginning or end, being the Great "I Am Who Am," Alpha and Omega, eternal.

- Humankind was created in the image of God.
- Both humans and animals received the breath of God.
- Humankind was uniquely created in the image of God by being given a soul.
- Animals were created as something wanted by God; they were given a *particular good.*
- All that God created was *good!*

6

Called to Stewardship of Creation

o o o o o o o o o o o o o o o o o o o o o o o o o o o o o o o o o o o o o o
Respect for laws inscribed in creation and the relations which derive from the nature of things is a principle of wisdom and a foundation for morality.[41]

Humankind, having been created by the breath of God and in the image of God, is called to a true and abiding friendship with God. This includes loving His whole creation in a truthful way by faithful imitation of God's love for all He has created. Through humankind, all of creation finds its destiny.

> "Heaven is my throne, and earth my footstool. What house will you build for me, says the Lord, or what is the place of my rest? Did not my hand make all these things?" (Acts 7:49–50)

God calls out to humankind's fidelity to govern creation with wisdom, compassion, and responsibility in response to God's love. And humanity is to respond as cooperators and good stewards because we are the recipient of such a great gift from the Creator.

Several psalms are attributed to King David. Perhaps he wrote this:

> When I look at thy heavens, the work of thy fingers, the moon and the stars which thou hast established; what is man that thou art mindful of him, and the son of man that thou dost care for him? Yet, thou hast made him little less than God, and dost crown him with glory and honor. Thou hast given him

dominion over the works of thy hand; thou hast put all things under his feet, all sheep and oxen, and also the beasts of the field, the birds of the air, and the fish of the sea, whatever passes along the paths of the sea. O Lord, our Lord how majestic is thy name in all the earth! (Ps. 8:3–8)

The Old Testament brings to words how great and wonderful are the works of God, who creates from nothingness and gives being and purpose to all creation:

The Lord has made everything for its purpose. (Prov. 16:4)

Humans, being given all things, move into covenant with God the Creator with all that is good. God gives to humans the perfect place of existence in the Garden of Eden. When Adam first resided in the garden, all of creation was domesticated and in perfect unity with its Creator. Nothing was imperfect, ill, hateful, carnivorous, or perverted. Loving God was the ultimate goal of all creatures as they worked together to serve Him and each other in the natural realm. Adam took care of the garden and tilled the ground for God, and all things glorified God perfectly. All was as God intended!

God then brought the animals so that Adam might name them.

Then the Lord God said, "It is not good that the man should be alone; I will make him a helper fit for him." So out of the ground the Lord God formed every beast of the field and every bird of the air, and brought them to the man to see what he would call them; and whatever the man called every living creature, that was its name. (Gen. 2:18–19)

You can allow yourself all the plausible reasons in the world why this would be included in sacred scripture, but there is only one definitive answer: God intended humankind to fulfill His design for the propagation of God's continued good in all creation. God gave to man a mission as a cooperator to the holy will: to name the animals.

God calls upon humankind to care for creatures with the same providential care that He has lovingly given. All of creation is subject to humans and affected by our love—or lack of love—for God.

The natural realm is forever changing through our choices of good or evil. Either we are in harmony with God, or we are not, and that choice is mirrored in creation. God placed on humankind the moral demand of obedience to His divine plan—and we have failed miserably. The fall of humankind occurred with the first sin. But that doesn't stop the love of the Creator to see us into redemption.

In the beginning, humans lived in harmony with God and with all of God's creation. There was no death, as sin had not yet entered the world. Humans had not yet moved into a broken relationship with their Creator. As the catechism says:

> Thus the revelation of creation is inseparable from the revelation and forging of the covenant of the one God with his People. Creation is revealed as the first step toward this covenant, the first and universal witness to God's all-powerful love.[42]

In summary:

- God entered into the first covenant He would have with man.
- All of creation—everything in the world—was given over to humans to care for by God.
- Man named all the animals.
- In response to God's love, humans were to govern creation with goodness and compassion, cooperating with God's holy will.

Interlude

o o o o o o o o o o o o o o o o o o o o o o o o o o o o o o o o o o o o
The birds reflect angelic likeness taking winged flight to the door of heaven, singing songs in the Creator's tongue, praising Him in words too foreign for man. Harken the sound of peace and harmony arising from the dark into morning's light, it is the quiet prayer of a tall standing tree and the whispered verse of a lily's bent head. Creator, created. But, where are the stewards?

—Susi Pittman

7

Sin Enters the World: Man and Creation Fall

○ ○

Law came in, to increase the trespass; but where sin increased, grace abounded all the more, so that, as sin reigned in death, grace also might reign through righteousness to eternal life through Jesus Christ our Lord.

—Romans 5:20–21

God created the first man, Adam, with a soul of free will and intellect that allowed Adam to choose freely to love and glorify his Creator. The soul separates the man, Adam, from all other animals, because he contains within himself the distinctive element of rationale. Man was created by God out of love, to be both material and soul, or spirit. The spiritual essence is what images God. Being made in the image of God, man is allowed to live eternally in special union with God.

God gave Adam's soul a supernatural existence such that death would not occur as long as Adam remained in harmonious covenant with God. Man does not have a spiritual likeness to any other creature, but only to God. All that Adam could have wanted was taken care of for him by God's providential care, even to the point of being given a human companion, whom Adam named Eve.

> Then the Lord God said, "It is not good that the man should be alone; I will make him a helper fit for him." (Gen. 2:18)

So the Lord God caused a deep sleep to fall upon the man,

and while he slept took one of his ribs and closed up its place with flesh; and the rib which the Lord God had taken from the man he made into a woman and brought her to the man. (Gen. 2:21–23)

God created a helpmate for Adam: a gender opposite, a female, the woman he named Eve. This difference in sex is made clear only as it regards the human creation. It seems important that humankind recognize the difference in male and female, masculine and feminine; yet not so for the animals. The animals were simply instructed to be fruitful and multiply, which adds to the argument that creatures are hardwired to understand their Creator. Man's free will needed divine instruction.

Saint Paul affirms the order in which man and woman are placed in God's creative flow:

For a man … is the image and glory of God; but woman is the glory of man. (For man was not made from woman, but woman from man. Neither was man created for woman, but woman for man.) (1 Cor. 11:7–10)

Woman was given to man to be a loving companion, and man, in turn, would care for her with the love God intended worthy of His creation. The Garden of Eden and its surroundings were given to be home to Adam and Eve by God, with only one commandment:

"You may freely eat of every tree of the garden; but of the tree of the knowledge of good and evil you shall not eat, for in the day that you eat of it you shall die." (Gen. 2:16–17)

Why do you think God gave Adam and Eve this commandment? Did God wish to place an undue obligation on man just so he would sin?

Of course not! God had given the humans a perfect existence, filled with His perfect love and providential care. And by giving Adam and Eve free will, He gave them the ultimate joy of choosing to love Him intimately in return, by being obedient to His authority as Creator.

Man and woman were surrounded with the perfection and beauty of all the created creatures and the fullness of creation.

And then the day came when Adam and Eve sinned against God, losing the harmony and the grace of original holiness.

We know that the prince of envy and pride—the ancient demon, Satan; the tempter; the enemy angel who opposes God—was the central player in this downfall. With the completion of the Garden of Eden, it wasn't long before Satan moved to despoil the beauty of all of God's creation, especially that special creature, man, who was created in the image of God. In the evil one's mind, how dare God create something so despicable and love it. Satan would have no part in it except to try and destroy it. At the beginning of time, Satan and other angels chose not to worship the Second Person of the Trinity, the Incarnate Word (Jesus). Pride was the reason for his fall from heaven, and his name was Satan, the enemy, who moved against God and rejected God's love. In response, God cast him out of heaven and into a place prepared for him: hell. The catechism says:

Scripture and the Church's tradition see in this being a fallen angel, called "Satan" or the "devil." The Church teaches that Satan was at first a good angel, made by God: "The devil and the other demons were indeed created naturally good by God, but they became evil by their own doing."[43]

For if God did not spare the angels when they sinned, but cast them into hell and committed them to pits of nether gloom to be kept until the judgment ... then the Lord knows how to rescue the godly from trial, and to keep the unrighteous under punishment until the day of judgment. (2 Pet. 2:4, 9)

To foil God's plan of beauty and goodness, Satan tempted Eve's free will by enticing her to be like God, to hold God in contempt, and to eat of the tree of good and evil. She believed what Satan said, and she ate. She then called upon Adam to taste and see, too, and he followed suit.

From the cause of this sin of disobedience came the effect of that sin: purity and innocence gave way to carnal lust and death.

Then the eyes of both were opened, and they knew that they were naked; and they sewed fig leaves together and made themselves aprons. (Gen. 3:7)

This act of disobedience brings an end to God's perfect world—innocence and beauty lost forever, a paradise tainted. God then promises that man and all generations forth will now suffer an earthly death, because sin has severed the perfect bond that once existed. Adam and Eve are told they will suffer death and return to the earth, no longer to be earthly immortals.

> "In the sweat of your face you shall eat bread till you return to the ground, for out of it you were taken; you are dust, and to dust you shall return." (Gen. 3:19)

When sin entered time through Adam and Eve, pain and death were initiated as the consequences of sin. This act of disobedience on their part also brought the effect of the fall to all of Creation. Humanity's disobedience caused the soul to be distorted, losing for us the harmony with our Creator that we had been given and bringing disharmony to all of creation before its God.

> Therefore the land mourns, and all who dwell in it languish, and also the beasts of the field, and the birds of the air; and even the fish of the sea are taken away. (Hosea 4:3)

Saint Bonaventure says that "humanity was blinded when it turned from the divine light to seek another good."[44] The harmony that was shared in a perfect existence ceased, and division was set between man and God, and all of creation with man. For as goes the way of man, so goes the way of all creation, which was made subject to man.

> For the creation waits with eager longing for the revealing of the sons of God; for the creation was subjected to futility not of its own will but by the will of him who subjected it in hope; because the creation itself will be set free from its bondage to decay and obtain the glorious liberty of the children of God. We know that the whole creation has been groaning in travail together until now. (Rom. 8:19–22)

As tragic as the fall of man was, Satan did not win. Satan has always been relegated to winning some skirmishes, but never the war. Satan is still just a creature, a created being, a mystery permitted by God. God would not let sin separate humankind and creation from Him. God, we must remember, is the most powerful existence in the universe. He has always been and always will be the One who brings a greater good from evil and suffering, a God who does not forget His covenants. The timeline for God's plan of salvation began immediately at the fall. It begins when God makes a promise to Satan the serpent:

"I will put enmity between you and the woman, and between your offspring and hers; He will strike at your head while you strike at his heel." (Gen. 3:15)

This was a foretelling that God would raise a new Eve, Mary, who would bear Jesus—the One destined to overcome Satan, redeeming man and all of His creation, and triumphantly striking Satan down forever at the end of time.

In summary:

- God created man to be perfect, without sin, and all of creation was pure.
- Man chose to disobey God and fell from grace, as did all creation with him.
- Death was the consequence of man's disobedience to God, not only for himself, but for all future generations and all of creation.
- Yet God does not let even sin separate man and creation from redemption.

8

Jesus Makes All Things New

o o o o o o o o o o o o o o o o o o o o o o o o o o o o o o o o o o o

For he has made known to us in all wisdom and insight the mystery of his will, according to his purpose which he set forth in Christ as a plan for the fullness of time, to unite all things in him, things in heaven and things on earth.

—Ephesians 1:9–10

God planned to save and to sum up all things in Christ Jesus, His Son. Jesus came to earth to bring redemption and salvation to all humankind; He suffered death by crucifixion only to resurrect in glory in three days, breaking the bonds of sin and death. Every person, by free will, can choose to receive this salvation or to reject it. Jesus, Son of God, took all human sin ever committed and ever to be committed, and received it unto Himself, that those who believe in Him would not perish but find redemption. He opened the door to God the Father that Adam had closed with original sin.

> Then as one man's trespass led to condemnation for all men, so one man's act of righteousness leads to acquittal and life for all men. ... Where sin increased, grace abounded all the more. (Rom. 5:18, 20)

Humankind can never merit eternity with God except to choose to receive the grace and salvation offered by Jesus, the Word.

Adam's soul—which, through sin, had distorted and alienated not only himself but the whole of creation from God—was without reconciliation. The sin of the first humans had broken the perfect

43

relationship with God. The door to heaven was closed. It is through Jesus made flesh, the Incarnate Word, that all of creation is renewed in covenant, and the door to heaven once again opens.

It is in Christ, Redeemer and Savior, that the divine image, disfigured in man by the first sin, has been restored to its original beauty and ennobled by the grace of God.[45]

As Jesus was the new Adam of the new covenant, Mary, Mother of Jesus, was the new Eve. The Word was made flesh through the Virgin Mary, who said yes to God and received the Word into her womb through the transcendent power of the Holy Spirit. Nothing in the history of the world can ever surpass the pre-eminent importance of this moment in all of time, when the world stood in hushed stillness to listen to the voice of a Jewish maiden, Mary, as she answered the angel of God and voiced her *fiat*.

"Do not be afraid, Mary, for you have found favor with God. And behold, you will conceive in your womb and bear a son, and you shall call his name Jesus. He will be great, and will be called the Son of the Most High ..."
And Mary said, "Behold, I am the handmaid of the Lord; let it be to me according to your word." (Luke 1:30–32, 38)

And the Word became flesh and dwelt among us, full of grace and truth; we have beheld his glory, glory as of the only Son from the Father. (John 1:14)

The Son of God was made visible; Jesus made this world His home, giving all creation a new dignity. Jesus, the eternal architect of creation, is wisdom and truth going before all creation as part of the Trinity, God in Three Persons.

When he established the heavens, I was there,
when he drew a circle on the face of the deep,
when he made firm the skies above,
when he established the fountains of the deep,
when he assigned to the sea its limit,

so that the waters might not transgress his command,
when he marked out the foundations of the earth,
then I was beside him, like a master workman;
and I was daily his delight,
rejoicing before him always,
rejoicing in his inhabited world
and delighting in the sons of men. (Prov. 8: 27–31)

He makes all things new again as the mediator of all creation. He is above all things! Wisdom dwells with humanity and creates a new pathway to God, the Father.

The human race and all of creation, which is intimately connected to and also reaches its destiny through humankind, will be enjoined together and face the coming renewal of all things when Jesus returns to bring about the promised new heavens and new earth.

There exists great hope for those creatures we love, who share our journey and serve us. Jesus has a great affinity with all that the Father has created, being the very One through whom all that was created entered into the world, and the One who will restore all things to eternal perfection!

Saint Paul describes the covenant of Christ with all of His creation. The sacrifice of Jesus on the cross before the whole world was the bringing of man and all creation out from death, and giving all the promise of a new and glorious life eternal with God:

He is the image of the invisible God, the first-born of all creation; for in him all things were created, in heaven and on earth, visible and invisible … He is before all things, and in him all things hold together. … For in him all the fullness of God was pleased to dwell, and through him to reconcile to himself all things, whether on earth or in heaven, making peace by the blood of his cross. (Col. 1:15–17, 19–20)

God's new covenant with the world was made manifest with the birth, life, death, resurrection, and ascension of His Son, Jesus—the perfect sacrifice for all time.

Man is saved by the grace and redemption that Jesus brings. So, too, is all of creation! Creatures and creation are brought to their perfect destiny as part of the redemptive act of Jesus, not only for man, but for the whole of creation.

> We know that the whole creation has been groaning in travail together until now; and not only the creation, but we ourselves who have the first fruits of the Spirit as sons. (Rom. 8:22–23)

Saint Francis of Assisi also believed that the incarnation of our Lord Jesus redeemed all of creation.[46] The redemption that occurred when Christ suffered, died, and was resurrected affected all of creation, resulting in not only humankind's but also creation's reconciliation with God. Christ created the new order; Christ is the new covenant.

> Therefore, if anyone is in Christ, he is a new creation; the old has passed away, behold, the new has come. All this is from God, who through Christ reconciled us to himself and gave us the ministry of reconciliation; that is, God was in Christ reconciling the world to himself. (2 Cor. 5:17–19)

> And he who sat upon the throne said, "Behold, I make all things new." (Rev. 21:5)

> But according to his promise we wait for new heavens and a new earth in which righteousness dwells. (2 Pet. 3:13)

> Because the creation itself will be set free from its bondage to decay and obtain the glorious liberty of the children of God. (Rom. 8:21)

Jesus opened the door for us to know the beatitude of heaven from whence the soul came, and for all of creation to be renewed and redeemed!

> Christ is Lord of the cosmos and of history. In him human history and indeed all creation are "set forth" and transcendently fulfilled.[47]

Jesus, God's definitive Word, the one priest of the new covenant, enters heaven and stands before God on behalf of man and all creation. He came to triumphantly undo Satan's work, making all things new again as the mediator of all creation. All things center on Christ, the Son of God made man.

My favorite scripture of God's providential intent for creation comes from the Book of Wisdom. It speaks of how very much God loves all that He has created, and how He sustains it and includes it in His saving plans.

> For thou lovest all things that exist, and hast loathing for none of the things which thou hast made, for thou wouldst not have made anything if thou hadst hated it. How would anything have endured if thou hadst not willed it? Or how would anything not called forth by thee have been preserved? Thou sparest all things, for they are thine, O Lord who lovest the living. For thy immortal spirit is in all things. (Ws. 11:24–26, 12:1)

Man, in his response to such love, exclaims from his soul a hymn of praise. That triumphant hymn of the angels, the "Trisagion," was first echoed by the prophet Isaiah:

> "Holy, holy, holy is the Lord of hosts;
> The whole earth is full of his glory." (Isa. 6:3)

The promised renewal that all of creation is earnestly awaiting has already begun in Jesus. He fulfilled the promise that nothing good would be lost, and that all good which God created from the beginning would find its home in Him and be made perfect.

In receiving Jesus as Savior, humanity is called to live a good life and to work for good. Jesus, the infinite source of love, the Beloved, remains our eternal source of communion. It will be before the eternal love, when we are judged, that God will ensure our complete and total happiness, whatever that may comprise.

In summary:

- The Word was made flesh and dwelt among humankind.
- The Incarnation of the Word redeemed man and all of the world.
- Jesus, by His life, death, resurrection, and ascension, set humanity and creation free from sin and death to consecrate it anew and return it to the Father for His glory.

9

Covenant: A God Who Promises!

o o o o o o o o o o o o o o o o o o o o o o o o o o o o o o o o o

Now therefore, if you will obey my voice and keep my covenant, you shall be my own possession among all peoples; for all the earth is mine, and you shall be to me a kingdom of priests and a holy nation.

—Exodus 19:5–6

Looking at the covenants of old and new helps us to see that God is not a liar. He promises, and He keeps all His promises. Man is the one who breaks his relationship with God. God has called man into covenants with Himself on many occasions; let's look at three particular covenants that truly relate to man and the animals.

It is in the glory of the Church that the God of covenant is profoundly acknowledged during the Mass in the recitation of the Eucharistic Prayer. Humans were called into their first covenant with God at their creation in the Garden of Eden. God created man and woman, male and female, in His image, to share in God's life and in God's omnipotent love. According to the catechism:

> By the radiance of this grace all dimensions of man's life were confirmed. As long as he remained in the divine intimacy, man would not have to suffer or die. The inner harmony of the human person, the harmony between man and woman, and finally the harmony between the first couple and all creation, comprised the state called "original justice.[48]

In creating humans, God gave them a soul (God's image) with which to love Him, and He made it a place of encounter and covenant because it is here that humanity uniquely images God. With each covenant that God made with humans, you can believe that He knew exactly the human He was dealing with. The covenant made with humanity and all of creation at the beginning of time was the sharing in the truth, beauty, goodness, and love of God.

The breaking of the covenant in the Garden of Eden arrived with Adam and Eve's disobedience to God. Adam and Eve fell to the sins of disobedience and pride, and man and all of creation has fallen into the dark chasm of death. I have often thought about what this world would have been like if sin had never entered in. I am sure that heaven holds that existence in a special place.

Yet God never abandoned His covenant with man and creation in the garden. He could have just let all that He had created end with Adam and Eve in sin and death. God could have annihilated this universe out of existence into nothingness! Our God, however, is a God of covenant! He is a God of promise! He proclaimed that what had been brought into existence was good, and He did not and will not abandon it.

Even at the dawn of creation, there existed the promise of a forthcoming redemption: the promise of Mary, the woman, who bears the Son of God; and Jesus saves humanity and creation from death and Satan—"he shall bruise your head" (Gen. 3:15).

The second covenant we look at reflects the very special relationship that God extended to Noah, all the animals, and the whole of creation.

The story of Noah is a terrific example of God's love for humankind and creatures, and the covenant he makes with both. I like who Noah was, and I like the fact that he was a "stand-alone" guy who didn't succumb to the pressures of the world and its ways.

In the time of Noah, the world had moved to a terrible and corrupted state because of the incalculable sins of humanity, and God was preparing to cleanse what He had created. The world had become so violent and full of immoral filth that God could no longer allow the rest of His creation to succumb to it. What was good, man called bad; what was bad, man called good: lying, killing, idol worship, adultery, profanity, sexual perversions, pride, disobedience, fornication, avarice, envy, desecration of what was holy, mercilessness, and bloodthirsty acts—which, I've got to say, sounds all too familiar. The cleansing would be a forthcoming justice unlike any in the history of the world: a flood to destroy everything on earth.

So where is God's love in that?

Lest we forget, humans, creation, and the universe were created out of eternal love to bring glory to God. The good rests in the preservation of Noah and his family, who lived their lives to glorify God, and in the preservation of all the animals that were under the divine providential care of God. It is here that we see God's desire to refresh the world in goodness once again. We can only imagine how evil the world must have been for God to be moved to such purification.

As He had done since the creation of the world, God moved forward with His plans for the redemption of mankind *and* creation. Noah was chosen by God because of who he was, a holy man, and his family would have the privilege of repopulating the world again. Noah's ancestral lineage was true to their Creator, a holy line of God's faithful people:

> Noah was a righteous man, blameless in his generation; Noah walked with God. (Gen. 6:9)

> God said to Noah and to his sons with him, "Behold, I establish my covenant with you and your descendants after you, and with every living creature that is with you." (Gen. 9:8–9)

Noah, never being one to "rock God's boat," was laughed at and scorned by the world as he built the massive ark that God had commissioned. He built the huge ship on dry land, trusting that God would deliver the rains of purification. Noah was a man of unimaginable faith, obeying God in every way, even though his actions appeared ridiculous to the rest of the world.

Noah was to gather a male and a female of every creature on the earth. (You might think to yourself, "Yeah, right! All those animals, all the food needs—not to mention the waste expulsion—and surely they would try and eat one another!") But remember, God can do anything He wants. And man in communion with God can accomplish things beyond physical, rational, and natural means. Believe me, if it was important to have an animal from halfway across the world in that ark, it was there; if there was to be enough to feed all the creatures and the humans, it was there; if there was to be harmony of all creation, it happened. All participants in this paramount moment were responding to their Creator the way the Creator had asked. It defied all probability and possibility!

Our rational selves today are so quick to discount the implausible as being impossible, and we forget our spiritual roots. Today the mantras of choice are logic (man thinking things out for himself), science (a group of men patting each other on the back, believing they have all the answers), and common sense (man must be able to see, touch, taste, hear, or smell something to believe it). Not so with Noah.

Noah was also instructed to bring his wife, his three sons, and his sons' wives. They would share the duties of caring for all the animals for what some scholars say was just over a year's time. The rains came and the entire world was engulfed in waters, purging its surface of all life.

The covenant that God made with Noah continues to the present day, and is a testimonial to the love of the Creator for man and all of the animals that received the breath of life from God. The floods came; and in time, the water subsided. God promises to never again cause a global destruction of life on earth by water. Man's contempt and self-justification in deifying himself above the Creator was destroyed, and a new era of covenant began.

"I will never again curse the ground because of man, for the imagination of man's heart is evil from his youth; neither will I ever again destroy every living creature as I have done." (Gen. 8:21)

"I establish my covenant with you, that never again shall all flesh be cut off by the waters of a flood and never again shall there be a flood to destroy the earth."

And God said, "This is the sign of the covenant which I make between me and you and every living creature that is with you, for all future generations: I set my bow in the cloud, and it shall be a sign of the covenant between me and the earth." (Gen. 9:12–13)

God chose to make the earth a new and better place for all His creation to once again flourish. All the animals would repopulate the world, as would the humans.

It would appear that it was at this time that the Lord put the fear of humans into the hearts of the animals. When I was younger, I had wondered, "When did man begin to eat the animals?" It is presumed in some circles of theology that man was a vegetarian until after the flood, after which he became carnivorous at some point.

At any rate, two verses in Genesis support the notion that humankind's relationship with animals changed after the flood:

"The fear of you and the dread of you shall be upon every beast of the earth, and upon every bird of the air, upon everything that creeps on the ground and all the fish of the sea; into your hand they are delivered. Every moving thing that lives shall be food for you; and as I gave you the green plants, I give you everything." (Gen. 9:2–3)

That the fear of man was placed in all creatures is echoed again in the collection of proverbs in the book of Sirach:

He placed the fear of them in all living beings, and granted them dominion over beasts and birds. (Sir 17:4)

The covenant God shared with Noah certainly worked out. Man and beast repopulated the world and, at least for a while, the world was a better place. God spoke of the visual sign, the rainbow, which He created to signify the covenant between Himself and all creation that there would never again be a global flood:

"When the bow is in the clouds, I will look upon it and remember the everlasting covenant between God and every living creature of all flesh that is upon the earth." (Gen. 9:16)

The third and final covenant I will address is the life, death, resurrection, and ascension of Jesus Christ—the new covenant! It is the most important covenant of all!

God's relationships and covenants recorded in the Old Testament find their fulfillment in the Word of God, the One who would make all things new, thus filling the redemptive cup to overflowing:

> "And we bring you the good news that what God promised to the fathers, this he has fulfilled to us their children by raising Jesus." (Acts 13:32–33)

> For if we have been united with him in a death like his, we shall certainly be united with him in a resurrection like his. … For we know that Christ being raised from the dead will never die again; death no longer has dominion over him. The death he died he died to sin, once for all, but the life he lives he lives to God. So you also must consider yourselves dead to sin and alive to God in Christ Jesus. (Rom. 6:5, 9–11)

Jesus told His disciples that He had brought forward the new covenant, and that He was the fulfillment of everything written about Him in the Mosaic law and the scriptures of the Old Testament.

> And he came to Nazareth, where he had been brought up; and he went to the synagogue, as his custom was, on the sabbath day. And he stood up to read; and there was given to him the book of the prophet Isaiah. He opened the book and found the place where it was written,
> > "The Spirit of the Lord is upon me, because he has anointed me to preach good news to the poor. He has sent me to proclaim release to the captives and recovering of sight to the blind, to set at liberty those who are oppressed, to proclaim the acceptable year of the Lord."
> And he closed the book, and gave it back to the attendant, and sat down; and the eyes of all in the synagogue were fixed on him. And he began to say to them, "Today this scripture has been fulfilled in your hearing."

> He learned obedience through what he suffered; and being made perfect he became the source of eternal salvation to all who obey him. (Heb. 5:8–9)

Jesus's death on the cross was necessary to renew the world and redeem the souls of the believers. Jesus came into this world to serve His Father, and to die in reparation for all the sins mankind would perpetrate throughout the ages.

> For as in Adam all die, so also in Christ shall all be made alive. But each in his own order ... Then comes the end, when he delivers the kingdom to God. (1 Cor. 15:22–24)

Christ's redemption brings all things from the time of Adam forward into alignment with their Creator. In the Garden of Eden, God asked man for his love and obedience. Once again He asks man to love and obey His Son, Jesus, the Christ:

> "No one has ascended into heaven but he who descended from heaven, the Son of man. And as Moses lifted up the serpent in the wilderness, so must the Son of man be lifted up, that whoever believes in him may have eternal life." (John 3:13–15)

Christ by His resurrection brings the hope of salvation to all of humanity in the new covenant, though each one of us must choose Him as our Savior. We today are a "new-covenant" people! As *Christ*-ians we are commissioned in His name to go forth and preach the gospel, doing good works as He commanded. He certainly never proclaimed that He was the Messiah, then sat around waiting for everybody to find Him. He attended to His Father's work every moment that He walked upon this earth.

Jesus also promises that man will be judged by his works at his particular death and at the end of time.

> Do you want to be shown, you foolish fellow, that faith apart from works is barren? Was not Abraham our father justified by works, when he offered his son Isaac upon the altar? You see that faith was active along with his works, and faith was completed by works. (James 2:20–22)

> So faith by itself, if it has no works, is dead. (James 2:17)

> Also another book was opened, which is the book of life. And the dead were judged by what was written in the books, by what they had done. (Rev. 20:12)

Living what He preached, Jesus worked here on earth eternally obedient to His Father in heaven, even unto the cross. He obeyed His Father in all things, allowing Himself to be baptized by John the Baptist as the outward sign of His acceptance of His mission to suffer and die.

> Now when all the people were baptized, and when Jesus also had been baptized and was praying, the heaven was opened, and the Holy Spirit descended upon him in bodily form, as a dove, and a voice came from heaven, "Thou art my beloved Son; with thee I am well pleased." (Luke 3:21–22)

I chose this scripture because of its visual content of the Holy Spirit in the bodily form of a dove. Isn't it a beautiful vision to call up in the mind's eye, a dove descending down upon the head of our Lord? Ponder the religious artwork on this subject. Why did the Holy Spirit come in that form? God in the Third Person could have taken any form, either ethereal or material. Perhaps it was a sign that none of Jesus's actions were absent from any of creation. The Holy Spirit in the form of a dove is a Christian symbol used consistently as a sign of receiving the Holy Spirit or the presence of the Holy Spirit.

Jesus asked us to be a "beatitude people" and to follow a simple, stewardship lifestyle—loving our fellow man and embracing the gifts that our Creator-Father has given us—as a way to reach heaven. Jesus expects nothing less of us but to tend this world as beatitude people working for the kingdom of God on earth.

The end of time draws closer and Jesus will bring to completion His redemptive act. Following the general resurrection and final judgment, the universe will be renewed and God's plan realized. All of creation is destined to be transformed and renewed through the one Jesus! Scripture tells us:

> The creation itself will be set free from its bondage to decay and

obtain the glorious liberty of the children of God. (Rom. 8:21)

We know that in everything God works for good. (Rom. 8:28)

The completion of the covenant of redemption of all creation is addressed at the end of the Bible in the book of Revelation. Satan has been working since the Garden of Eden to bring humanity and as much of creation as possible to ruin before he is eternally locked away with all of his demons and the lost souls. He is especially hard at work in today's world; we witness the violence directed at, the war upon, the destruction of, and the merciless artificial manipulation of humankind and creation. Yet the covenant of redemption promises that all good that was begun will end through Jesus, while what is evil will be doomed to ruin.

God is the One who always existed, the perfect circle, without end. He is with us in covenant until the end of time, when Jesus will judge all.

Then I saw a great white throne and him who sat upon it; from his presence earth and sky fled away and no place was found for them. And I saw the dead, great and small, standing before the throne, and books were opened. Also another book was opened, which is the book of life. (Rev. 20:11-12)

And just as it is appointed for men to die once, and after that comes judgment. (Heb. 9:27)

Man will be brought to a judgment that will be carried out in the just tempest of a righteous God who allows creation to play its role.

Then I saw an angel standing in the sun, and with a loud voice he called to all the birds that fly in midheaven, "Come, gather for the great supper of God, to eat the flesh." (Rev. 19:17)

The earth and all of creation will be in convulsions as man arrives at the brink of an evil destruction. God will then intervene.

As it was in the days of Noah, so will it be in the days of the Son of man. (Luke 17:26)

"It is done!" And there were flashes of lightning, loud noises, peals of thunder, and a great earthquake such as had never been since men were on the earth, so great was that earthquake. And every island fled away, and no mountains were to be found; and great hailstones, heavy as a hundredweight, dropped on men from heaven, till men cursed God for the plague of the hail, so fearful was that plague. (Rev. 16:17-18, 20-21)

The world will be brought to its end at the final judgment, when all will stand before God and either receive eternal reward or eternal damnation, and Satan will be cast into hell forever. That alone helps me want to live a better life. The thought of being separated from my God—who promises me eternal joy in His kingdom where all good is brought to its perfected end—is unbearable. I rejoice in God's promise, which we find in Revelation:

Then I saw a new heaven and a new earth; for the first heaven and the first earth had passed away, and the sea was no more. (Rev. 21:1)

And he who sat upon the throne said, "Behold, I make all things new." (Rev. 21:5)

I love this great and glorious promise from Jesus, who will indeed bring all that is good into its true beauty for all eternity! It is here, in this scripture, where I find myself embracing all that I have loved in creation, and hope to share with it anew in Jesus's kingdom! We and all of creation are no longer condemned to death!

The covenant between God and man that began in the Garden of Eden is still the covenant God asks us to honor today by being good stewards of all that He has given us. What wonder and awe we have to look forward to as followers of Jesus, to share in His glory and works forever!

Part III
The Way of the Soul

10

Understanding The Soul

"My soul magnifies the Lord, and my spirit rejoices in God my Savior"

—Luke 1:4

This chapter, above all others, caused me to research into the wee hours of the night to pull together something so sacred and sensitive to us all. What is a soul? What is the human soul? Do animals have souls? What is the general end for all things?

The first chapter of Genesis states that God initiated His creative act by sending out the Spirit, the breath of God, across the waters and into all creatures, calling them good. We read in the catechism:

> It belongs to the Holy Spirit to rule, sanctify, and animate creation, for he is God, consubstantial with the Father and the Son. ... Power over life pertains to the Spirit, for being God he preserves creation in the Father through the Son.[49]

It is because of this that the revelation and likeness of God is universal in creation around the world in the language of creatures. Like a mirror to the face of God, creation is given its dignity, and it both inspires and leads humankind to the awesome beauty of love's true nature, God.

> All creatures bear a certain resemblance to God, most especially man, created in the *image* and likeness of God. The manifold perfections of creatures—their truth, their goodness, their beauty—all reflect the infinite perfection of

God. Consequently we can name God by taking his creatures' perfections as our starting point, "for from the greatness and beauty of created things comes a corresponding perception of their Creator."[50]

God is Father and Creator, and it is through this omnipotence that God is in the creature and the creature is in Him. He gives all living things a transcendent dignity of being. There is, however, a definite distinction between human and nonhuman. To fully understand the truth of this division requires the ability to understand the differential.

The Catholic Encyclopedia defines the human soul as follows:

The soul may be defined as the ultimate internal principle by which we think, feel, and will, and by which our bodies are animated.[51]

The *Catechism of the Catholic Church* states this with regard to the human soul:

The Church teaches that every spiritual soul is created immediately by God—it is not "produced" by the parents—and also that it is immortal: it does not perish when it separates from the body at death, and it will be reunited with the body at the final Resurrection.[52]

The soul gives to us an immortal existence in the next life. It is unique to the human creature, and it unites us to our Creator in a way that is set apart from all animals. Does this mean that the rest of creation is not provided for in some way by God? No. What it does mean is that humans were created in the image of God; we receive a spiritual principle, being given intellect and free will.

What God gives cannot be taken away except by a deliberate act of refusal. Man is the only creature in creation that has the ability to refuse God's love.

Animals and the rest of creation do not have that ability. God has provided for them differently, creating them with their own *particular* good.

11

Man: Breath of God—Image of God

Then the Lord God formed man of dust from the ground, and breathed into his nostrils the breath of life; and man became a living being.

—Genesis 2:7

The breath of God—the Holy Spirit, which is the breath of life—is the life-giving force that animates the world. For example, when someone ceases to breathe, cardiopulmonary resuscitation (CPR) is usually performed. That act of saving, the very breath given in CPR, is beautifully analogous to what God does when He breathes the breath of life into His creatures. God's breath is saving and life-giving. It flows not only into man, but into all living creatures and creation and is sustained by the Holy Spirit.

The human soul is the spiritual principle of man imaging God and God giving man eternal qualities.

Then God said, "Let us make man in our image, after our likeness." (Gen. 1:26)

The soul is created only by God for God, and not by the procreative act of humans.[53] Each human receives only one soul that is destined to journey on earth, moving either toward or away from his Creator by his choices of right or wrong. We do not receive multiple return trips to earth to "get it right." The gift of "created being" is given only once.

Humans, as adopted brothers and sisters of Christ, were created to occupy a place lower than the angels, but higher than the animals.

"Thou hast made him for a little while lower than the angels— putting everything in subjection under his feet." (Heb. 2:7-8)

By imaging God, humankind is given knowledge, intellect, and a choice for an eternal existence—whether it is in heaven or in hell.

This makes us distinctly different from the rest of created creatures, both angels and animals. Humans live a life exercising free will, making constant moral decisions that affect not only the world and others about us, but also our mission on earth and our destiny with God. And we share differently in our eternal existence in heaven than do other creatures, since at the general resurrection, we are given a glorified persona—a body and soul perfectly united.

"But the King of the universe will raise us up to an everlasting renewal of life, because we have died for his laws." (2 Macc. 7:9)

"For the hour is coming when all who are in the tombs will hear his voice and come forth, those who have done good, to the resurrection of life, and those who have done evil, to the resurrection of judgment." (John 5:28–29)

If the Spirit of him who raised Jesus from the dead dwells in you, he who raised Christ Jesus from the dead will give life to our mortal bodies also through his Spirit who dwells in you. (Rom. 8:11)

The soul exists both naturally and supernaturally. Naturally, it is united to a body; supernaturally it is separated from its body. The soul separates from the body at death. It leaves its earthly container and goes to stand before Jesus for the particular judgment. The human soul and body are eternally connected; both will be reunited with Christ in glory, at the end of time, to be given a glorified being:

The body is not meant for immortality, but for the Lord, and the Lord for the body. And God raised the Lord and will also raise us up by his power. Do you not know that your bodies are members of Christ? (1 Cor. 6:13–14)

The human soul makes us rational beings. We use reason to acquire our knowledge, and intellect to address our free will. The body is the way in which human beings sense the world and all that is around them. The body isn't so much necessary to house the soul as it is important to our ability to experience the world.

The soul never perishes, as we are called to share by knowledge and love in the beatific vision. A human is not a some*thing*, but rather a some*one* who, through Jesus, is given a place as an adopted son or daughter before the Father. Through Jesus, we can enter into the glory of heaven and receive the inheritance promised to Him.

Humans most closely resemble God when we imitate God's love. The mind gives to us the ability to sense, understand, and love God— though imperfectly, until we arrive in heaven. Humankind lives in a world in which our senses enable us to enjoy the effects of colors and sounds, the majesty of the mountains, the vastness of the seas, and the magnificence of the cosmos overhead. How much can we love God back in return for all the beauty that surrounds us?

The heart is the place of encounter with God, as the soul yearns to be touched by the Creator's love. Some of our Catholic saints have been struck deeply by our Lord, and books have been written on their mystical encounters with the Lord. Saint Anne Emmerich, Saint Catherine of Siena, and Therese of Lisieux are excellent examples.

I feel I bore witness to the mystical encounter of my husband, Greg, into the hands of Jesus at Greg's death in our home. He drew his last breath and his body shone a golden glow witnessed by all in the room. Greg's desire always had been to love his Lord more and more as his days were shortened. This "glow" was followed by a distinct sense of "presence" about us, with a very definitive peace that remains in that room today. It was to us, in a sense, a parting gift of love.

And the dust returns to the earth as it was, and the spirit returns to God who gave it. (Eccles. 12:7)

The knowledge in our minds remains as we pass into death. Our love—or lack thereof—and our free-will choices will either guide us toward the glory of heaven, or to the eternal damnation of hell. We don't just flit out of our bodies and decide where we will flit off to next. We have a date with destiny that calls us before Jesus.

> For we must all appear before the judgment seat of Christ, so that each one may receive good or evil, according to what he has done in the body. (2 Cor. 5:10)

When we stand before holiness, will we find ourselves moving toward it, or being repulsed and running from it?

That process is taking place right now as we live and breathe and make our daily decisions. Our life actions become a scale that will either lift us up to glory, or weigh us down to hell.

But what about God's other creatures, the animals? Do they have a soul? Do they go before God at death? Are they given an eternal existence with God their Creator?

12

Animals: Breath of God

o o o o o o o o o o o o o o o o o o o o o o o o o o o o o o o o o o o
*For the fate of the sons of men and the fate of beasts is the same;
as one dies, so dies the other. They all have the same breath, and
man has no advantage over the beast; for all is vanity. All go to
one place; all are from the dust, and all turn to dust again. Who
knows whether the spirit of man goes upward and the spirit of the
beast goes down to the earth?*

—Ecclesiastes 3:19–21

The opening scripture for this chapter is a great one! Who knows the
answer to the question Ecclesiastes raises? Only God!

Animals and humans were touched by the first principle of life,
which is the Holy Spirit—the breath of life. Man and nonhuman
creatures were created on the same day and given their particular order
before God.

Animals and man were created with condition, form, and order.
Their condition is that they are created from a source of love; they
exist in a form created from the Word of God; they exist in a functional
order as willed by the love of God.

Animals do not sin. They were not created as rational creatures;
they do not use an intellect to make moral choices, nor do they choose
to sin.

Animals operate within the natural law that was ordered to them
by God. What life they are predisposed to here on earth is generated by
God's steward of creation, humankind.[54]

Animals do have feelings. Are those feelings caused by chemical
responses similar to those that human beings experience, or are

humans guilty of anthropomorphism—putting human motivations on animals? Animals are not unfeeling objects. A recent study done at Oxford on animal behavior showed that animals do experience a range of emotions.[55]

Animals do not have the particular immortal soul that man has. They were given a *particular good* that guarantees their return to the One who created them. The image of God was reserved for humans,…. and the animals, by their design, were reserved first for God, and then for humans. All things deriving from God are ordered to one another and to Him, and will find their final perfection and rest in Him.

Jesus says:
"All that the Father gives me will come to me." (John 6:37)

Just because animals do not have an immortal soul as man has does not mean that they don't have an eternal continuance by divine providence upon death, or that God cannot raise them up when the universe is recreated at the general resurrection, or that they cannot be a part of our eternal happiness. We cannot be so arrogant as to put limits on the almighty providence of the Creator.

Animals did receive the breath of life and share uniquely in God's mystery of redemption for creation. Keeping in mind that God loves all that He has created and provides for each creature accordingly, there is nothing He creates that is in vain. Everything is preserved, as the following scripture tells us:

How greatly to be desired are all his works, and how sparkling they are to see! All these things live and remain forever for every need, and are all obedient. All things are twofold, one opposite the other, and he has made nothing incomplete. One confirms the good things of the other, and who can have enough of beholding his glory? (Sir 42:22–25)

Why would God, who loves us so much in our humanity, deprive us of anything that would only continue our happiness in eternity?

An animal is an animal, unique in its creation and different from man. The way that an animal is called to exist by God determines the way it will act. Truth be told, there was no one creature that could contain the love and goodness of God, so He filled the world with a marvelous array of creatures. That alone stands in testimony to the probability that God indeed has prepared an eternity especially for these creatures of His love and goodness!

By design, all nonhuman creatures exist to reflect the glory of God, and all will return to their Creator; you can bet on that, though how or when is a mystery for now. According to the catechism:

> We firmly believe that God is master of the world and of its history. But the ways of his providence are often unknown to us. Only at the end, when our partial knowledge ceases, when we see God "face to face," will we fully know the ways by which—even through the dramas of evil and sin—God has guided his creation to that definitive Sabbath rest for which he created heaven and earth.[56]

As man goes, so goes the whole of creation. Man's sins down through the ages have certainly affected animal behavior, reflecting man's own worst—and best—behaviors. Man and the lesser brethren are interconnected by the character and effect of human actions. We see in much of nature how brutal and murderous animals can be, one to another, predator and prey.

Yet, reflecting also the good effect of human actions, there are animal miracles where animals interdependently aid one another and man. There is still good in the world, and so the natural realm can still radiate goodness and hope.

A recent YouTube video of a dog being struck while crossing the interstate with another dog wrung my heart. But oh, the awesome moment of courage as the other dog returned to the highway to grab ahold of its friend and drag it away from any further harm.[57] Was God's love moving in His creature as it rescued its fellow creature? Was there a message to us in that action?

Jane Goodall, the famous chimpanzee expert, said, "We have to understand we are not the only beings on this planet with personalities and minds."[58]

God loves the nonhuman, non-rational creatures as things wanted by Him, and His desire is for man to share in them. Sometimes we share common habits.

Among our domestic pets, we can certainly see that this is true. Dogs do smile, and wiggle about, their mouths wide with the corners wrinkled up, as it were, exhibiting body language that's hard to ignore. Aren't we like that in happy social settings? Some of us more than others! I find it fitting that the Latin word for faithful is *fido*.

Cats can exhibit a zest for life! They zoom through the room at ninety miles an hour, stop at zero, and then off to yet another invisible location, with ears pinned back! Plain and simple, this is a cat's love of life manifested in exuberant motion. Now I wish I could say that humans who zoomed around in their cars at ninety miles an hour were doing so out of exuberance, but we know differently!

Domestic birds will chirp and sing cheerfully when their owner arrives home, sometimes even hearing the car before it enters the driveway or the footsteps coming up the walk, and they give, for all practical purposes, a spontaneous alert and loving welcome. Don't we humans love spontaneously singing along to iTunes?

All creation entered this world through Jesus, and every living piece of human and nonhuman creation will exit through Jesus. Only one creature will be judged, and that is man. God's providence has provided for the rest, though that is a mystery for now.

> We know that in everything God works for good for those who love him. (Rom. 8:28)

We read earlier about studies that offer proof that animals do experience emotions, which would thus lend itself to the scripture above. Humankind and animals can love God. We acknowledge that there is value and life in all that God creates, and that animals exist in our world because of God's great goodness and love for us. They share in the mystery of a creation that is powerfully united to its Creator. He looks after them in general and in particular; nothing escapes His providence.

The Holy Spirit is the divine sustaining power and the source of all life, being the breath of life. And we see that Jesus redeems all creation, making all things new! Earlier I shared how those who have had NDEs have seen and touched their family pets on the other side. Perhaps our pets are already in heaven, when you consider that the continued sustaining of all things by the Holy Spirit is a continuous source of conservation by God.

Psalm 104 is one of the most beautiful hymns of praise to God's creative power. It acknowledges that it is the Holy Spirit who sustains all His creatures:

> When thou sendest forth thy Spirit, they are created; and thou renewest the face of the ground. (Ps. 104:30)

Our God and Father loves all that He has created, right down to the smallest of creatures. He has ordered the universe and all His creatures, planning and providing for them, keeping all in His providential care. His heavenly providence sees all!

In Luke, we read:

> "Are not five sparrows sold for two pennies? And not one of them is forgotten before God." (Luke 12:6)

If God does not forget the least of creation, how can we say that He would forget what has been fostered by our love and His?

If all is from God, shouldn't we trust how He has structured creatures, and how He will handle their lives and their deaths?

Isn't it illogical to believe that God would find worthless that which is "hardwired" to give Him praise?

All things—including both human and beast—have their appointed time to live and to die. All things, including our beloved animal companions, rest in the eternal and providential hands of their Creator/Father! In Ecclesiastes, we read:

> For everything there is a season, and a time for every matter under heaven ... I know that whatever God does endures forever; nothing can be added to it, nor anything taken from it; God has made it so." (Eccles. 3:1, 14).

Man is the only created being that needs to be in conformity with his Creator, thereby fulfilling in creation his mission from God.

The implications of the following great scriptural exhortation leaves none of creation out, and acknowledges the glorious end of man, the animals, and all of creation. All of us, all of creation is ultimately on a final journey toward God!

> And I heard every creature in heaven and on earth and under the earth and in the sea, and all therein, saying, "To him who sits upon the throne and to the Lamb, be blessing and honor and glory and might for ever and ever!" (Rev. 5:13)

Part IV
Saints and the Animals

13

Saint Francis and the Animals

1181 to 1226
Patron Saint of Animals

Saint Francis of Assisi is one of the best known and most beloved of the beautiful Catholic saints. He is a Catholic saint who crosses the boundaries of all Christian faiths and one who embodies the kind and eternally loving Christ. He is not a New Age Peter Pan, embodying the realms of magic, earth worship, and a "me-centered" universe. His way was the gospel way of life in a world that was growing cold; he gave his entire being to Christ. The beautiful soul of Saint Francis sings of redemption for the world and touches the heart as only the truly blessed of God can.

I can't help but notice how popular the Saint Francis garden statues are among people's yards and gardens. It just seems right to have Saint Francis standing amid the flora and fauna of creation, hands extended to God's creatures in love. No matter their genus, he called them all brothers and sisters, and all of creation responded in kind to him.

We don't often think of the inanimate things of creation—the rocks, minerals, water, fire, and so on—as being brothers and sisters, but Saint Francis did. He was quick to give admiration to the beauty of a sunny day or the way the water glistens in the moonlight. All these things, too, are part of God's divine spark and reflect His love.

There was a time in Saint Francis's life when his eyesight was diminishing, and total blindness loomed on the horizon. He went to get help from a doctor who chose to cauterize his temple with a hot iron in hopes of a cure. As the iron was heated in the fire, Saint Francis addressed the fire as a brother, asking him for his goodness and not to burn him more than he could stand. Saint Francis was neither burned nor suffered any pain through the entire procedure. Can you imagine the astonishment of the doctor and the people who witnessed this? Can you imagine your own astonishment at such a happening? Who among us would be so confident as to ask the element of fire to "spare us pain"? Such confidence requires a great spiritual state of being, empty of oneself and filled with holiness, which Saint Francis indeed personified!

The greatness of "The Canticle of Brother Sun" is that it underscores the sacredness with which Saint Francis viewed all of creation because of its origin in the divine spark. He wrote the canticle towards the end of his life following a moment of supernatural spontaneity. In the canticle, Saint Francis emphasizes that all creation makes up the one family of God, and he invites praise to their Creator.

"The Canticle of Brother Sun"
Most high, all-powerful, all good, Lord!
All praise is yours, all glory, all honor
And all blessing.
To you alone, Most High, do they belong.
No mortal lips are worthy
To pronounce your name.
All praise be yours, my Lord, through all that
you have made,
And first my lord Brother Sun,
Who brings the day; and light you give to us
through him.
How beautiful is he, how radiant in all his
splendor!
Of you, Most High, he bears the likeness.
All praise be yours, my Lord, through Sister Moon
and Stars;
In the heavens you have made them, bright
And precious and fair.
All praise be yours, my Lord, through Brothers
Wind and Air,
And fair and stormy, all the weather's moods,
By which you cherish all that you have made.

All praise be yours, my Lord, through Sister Water,
    So useful, lowly, precious, and pure.
All praise be yours, my Lord, through Brother Fire,
    Through whom you brighten up the night.
How beautiful he is, how gay! Full of power
    And strength.
All praise be yours, my Lord, through Sister Earth,
    our mother,
Who feeds us in her sovereignty and produces
Various fruits and colored flowers and herbs.
All praise be yours, my Lord, through those who
    grant pardon
For love of you; through those who endure
    Sickness and trial.
Happy those who endure in peace,
By you, Most High, they will be crowned.
All praise be yours, my Lord, through Sister Death,
    From whose embrace no mortal can escape.
Woe to those who die in mortal sin!
Happy those She finds doing your will!
The second death can do no harm to them.
Praise and bless my Lord, and give him thanks,
    And serve him with great humility.
(An Englsih translation from the original Italian version, "Il Cantico
    del Sole") [59]

One of the most famous stories of the loving power of Saint Francis comes to us from the town of Gubbio, Italy. A wolf, driven by hunger, was terrorizing the town by killing and devouring not only domestic animals, but also townspeople. Saint Francis came to the aid of the town by volunteering to be their diplomat of peace. He went to the lair of the wolf to negotiate a deal.

Saint Francis said, "Brother Wolf, you have done great harm in this region, and you have committed horrible crimes by destroying God's creatures without any mercy."

Saint Francis told the wolf that the people promised to feed him every day, and in return, the wolf had to promise to never again destroy any creature or person in the town. The wolf gestured his agreement by bowing his head and placing his paw in the hand of Saint Francis. The wolf spent the remainder of his life being loved by the townspeople, who all fed the wolf from their homes. He was so loved by the people that at his death, the people mourned.[60]

The act of forgiveness given by the townspeople to the wolf brought forth the fruit of peace and holiness, and acted as a force even in creation. The wolf's peaceful ways were a constant reminder of the sanctity of Saint Francis, who tamed the wolf with love alone.

Today in Gubbio, you can visit a bronze relief of the wolf commemorating this event just a bit south of the *via di Frate Lupo*, which translates as "Brother Wolf Street." [61]

Catholicism recognizes the beauty in what Saint Francis preached on creation, and it honors him every year with his own feast day, October 4, at which time the Blessing of the Animals takes place. It is hard to find a Catholic parish on the Sunday nearest October 4 that does *not* offer this beautiful event!

An entire rite exists just for animals. If you haven't taken your beloved companion to one yet, don't miss the opportunity on the next October 4 to let your pet be blessed in this gracious way!

14

Saint John Bosco and Grigio

1815 to 1888
Patron Saint of Young Children

Saint John Bosco is perhaps one of the most gifted theologians in history. Because he was given the gift of dreams and visions, his life existed on both the natural and supernatural levels.

Saint John Bosco founded the Salesian Society, and was called by God to care for and teach the catechism to the rowdy, destitute, and neglected boys of his time, starting with his own village. He built oratories to educate them, and later expanded his curriculum to include teaching these young ruffians a trade, such as shoemaking or tailoring. His highest objective was to bring new priests to Christ through the Salesian order. The order also conducted educational programs for impoverished girls. [62]

God gave to Saint John Bosco a mysterious dog that became the protector of this great saint for much of his life. Where the dog came from and where it went was of no consequence to the saint; he genuinely accepted the friendship of the dog as part of divine providence.

Saint John Bosco did so much good saving the young boys of his time that I am sure it was the influence of the devil that riled people up against him, sometimes to the point that jealousy and hatred led men to try to kill the saint on more than one occasion. It was in response to that danger that a huge gray dog appeared one day when Saint John Bosco was being threatened by murderers. The dog, fearsome to behold, was described as a German shepherd standing three feet tall. Grigio, as he was named by Saint John Bosco, would always appear where trouble waited for the saint. When these ne'er-do-wells finally stopped trying to hurt Saint John Bosco, the dog disappeared. He appeared only one other time, when the saint was lost, to lead him safely to a Salesian home.[63]

Was the dog a wandering wolf who just irrationally took it upon himself to play protector to Saint John Bosco? Or was the dog perhaps sent from heaven? Many asked Saint John Bosco what happened to the dog, to which the saint was said to have responded, "What does it matter? It was my friend." [64] This was truly an expression of confidence in the reciprocal friendship between humans and animals accorded them by their Creator!

15

Saint Anthony of Padua and the Animals

1195 to 1231
Patron Saint of Horses

Saint Anthony, a devoted disciple of Saint Francis of Assisi, was born to a Portuguese family. He took the surname of Padua as an adult in honor of the many years of his life that he spent in that lovely Italian city. God blessed him with a brilliant mind, a magnetic personality, a bold voice, and a burning zeal for the salvation of souls. He also connected with animals on a level similar to that of Saint Francis of Assisi, united in spiritual brotherhood to his mentor.

Saint Anthony was in the town of Rimini, which was suffering under a large group of heretics and evildoers. He tried to preach the faith of Jesus to them, but his words fell on deaf ears. So Saint Anthony went to the river that joined the sea and called forth all the fish to hear the word of God. A great multitude of fish began to appear and line up as far as the eye could see, their heads popped up out of the water, listening to Saint Anthony speak. He told them of God's goodness in preserving them during the great flood, and of God's continued providential care for them. The townspeople saw this miracle and called others to come and witness what was happening. Soon the shoreline was full of people, including the heretics and evildoers. The saint preached to people and fish alike, and converted the heretics! Saint Anthony dismissed the fish, which left in complete peace and harmony with one another, swimming back into the depths of the river and out to the sea. [65]

On another occasion, Saint Anthony was called upon in a most extraordinary way to prove the real presence of our Lord Jesus' body and blood, soul, and divinity, in the Holy Eucharist (the Blessed Sacrament).

A well-known heretic challenged the saint with what he thought was a well-thought-out plan to dupe the credibility of the Blessed Sacrament. He certainly didn't believe that bread could be transubstantiated into the body of Jesus, so he masterminded what he thought was a foolproof plan. He would starve his donkey for three days, knowing full well the little donkey would choose to eat rather than respond to anything else. He would then bring the donkey to the town square and place a bale of hay a short distance away. [66]

During the three days that the heretic was starving the poor little donkey, Saint Anthony retreated to the forest to fast and pray.

On the appointed day, the villagers gathered at the square, and the donkey was led in amidst much fanfare. Saint Anthony also returned to town, went to the Church, took out the Blessed Sacrament, and arrived at the square.

The donkey was untied, and it began to advance toward the bale of hay. Saint Anthony held high the exposed Blessed Sacrament in the monstrance before all who had gathered, and before the donkey, saying, "Mule, in the name of the Lord our God, I command you to come here and adore your Creator!"[67]

The donkey stopped immediately, then turned and rushed to Saint Anthony. The donkey then bent his forelegs and bent his head down to the ground, genuflecting in adoration of the Blessed Sacrament.

The heretic was astonished! He then approached Saint Anthony to ask for forgiveness, and was converted.[68]

It was the address of Saint Anthony to the little donkey that celebrates the brotherhood of all creation: "in the name of the Lord *our* God."

16

Saint Germaine Cousin and the Sheep

1579 to 1601
Patron Saint of Poverty

This sweet saint was born in France with a weak body, a withered right hand, and sores on her neck, yet she was gifted with the sense of the *presence of God*. [69] From a very young age, she was a shepherdess, tending the family's sheep from morning until night. She was brutally treated by her stepmother, who forced her to sleep in the stable amid the farm animals, and who fed her only scraps. The saint's heart of love led her to share what scraps she had with the town beggars. [70]

She loved being out in nature, communing with God in the pastoral surroundings of her village. She also loved Jesus very much and did not want to miss a single daily Mass, so she would take the sheep with her to church. She would place her staff in the ground outside the church, and the sheep would remain until she returned. Her love for these creatures was so strong that, through the power of divine providence, never were her sheep attacked by the wolves that lived in great numbers around the town of Pibrac, nor did she ever lose a sheep. [71]

She died at the age of twenty-two, but her fervor for Mass and the Holy Eucharist, and her love of God's creatures, have been long remembered in her village of Pibrac, France. [72] Documents attest to over four hundred miracles attributed to her intercessions. [73]

17

Saint Roch and the Dog

1295 to 1327
Patron Saint of Dogs and Dog Lovers

Saint Roch, or Saint Rocco, was born in 1295 in Montpelier, France, to a wealthy French nobleman. Saint Roch was gifted with great social conscience and grew into maturity with a burning desire to help the poor, the sick, and the homeless. Could it be that the red birthmark on his chest, which was in the shape of a cross, was a visual harbinger of this saint's greatness to come?[74]

Saint Roch made a pilgrimage to Rome to care for the victims of a plague, healing them by the sign of the cross until he became infected himself. He left the city and retreated into the forest, where he lay dying.

A dog befriended him, licking the wounds of Saint Roch and bringing him fresh rolls from his master's house. The dog's master followed the dog one day and found Saint Roch, who he took into his care and helped to recover.[75]

Saint Roch and the dog left to return to France, where civil war was raging. No one recognized him, because he was emaciated from his illness. Sadly, his uncle, who was the governor at the time, did not recognize his own nephew. Saint Roch was wrongly accused of spying, and he and the dog were thrown into prison. During the five years that followed, he and his dog cared for the other prisoners and Saint Roch prayed and shared the word of God with them until the saint's death in 1327. [76] Numerous miracles followed his death. [77]

Catholic dog lovers are encouraged to seek the intercession of Saint Roch for their beloved pets. Saint Roch is represented in statuary in pilgrim garb accompanied by a dog carrying a loaf of bread in its mouth.[78]

18

Saint Rita of Cascia and the White Bees

1381 to 1457
Patron Saint of the Impossible

Saint Rita was five days old when beautiful white bees arrived to buzz about the little child's mouth and lips. The bees never harmed her, according to her mother and other witnesses. Saint Rita grew up to become a wife and mother, but she lost both her husband and her two sons to death.[79]

During Saint Rita's life at the convent of Cascia, a swarm of white bees took up residence in a fissure in the wall of the convent. The bees are still in the wall today. These bees hibernate for ten months of the year, emerging for Holy Week preceding Easter Sunday each year. They are never seen to leave the convent enclosure.[80] They remain around the gardens and the convent rooms for about two months, then return to the ancient wall after the feast of Saint Rita each May 22, sealing themselves into the holes they've made for another ten months.[81]

The bees were submitted as evidence for sainthood to Pope Urban VIII who did indeed beatify Saint Rita. Unusually true, was that the Pope's family coat of arms and his Papal Coat of Arms both held the image of three bees. Saint Rita's bodily remains have remained uncorrupted to the present day. [82]

19

Saint Francis Xavier and the Crab

1506 to 1552
Patron Saint of Missionaries

Saint Francis Xavier was the first great missionary to the Orient in modern times. He was born fourteen years after Columbus had made his first voyage. [83]

One of the great miracle stories about Saint Francis Xavier is how he got his crucifix back after losing it at sea.

A terrible storm had arisen while Saint Francis was traveling aboard a ship bound for Baranura. Saint Francis Xavier held up his crucifix into the wind and the storm asking God to quell it. The seas were calmed. However, the crucifix slipped from the saint's hands and fell into the ocean.

Saint Francis arrived safely in Baranura. When he disembarked and was walking along the shoreline, a very large crab made its way out of the sea, and in his claw was Saint Francis's crucifix. The crab gave it to the saint and returned to the sea, but not before Francis had prayed in thanksgiving. This was witnessed and attested to in historical records.[84]

Though the story may be hard for some to believe, this event was accepted by the Vatican as one of three miracles for the canonization of Saint Francis Xavier. The story was depicted on the altar at the canonization ceremony and was one of the four miracles on a banner decorating St. Peter's Church. [85]

The crab species of this story carries a distinct sign of the cross on its back and still exists in the Straits of Malacca where Portugese fishermen believe them to be holy and will not eat them. [86]

Part V
Personal Animal Miracles

20

The Dutch Girl

The greatest dog in the world lived at my house! How many of us can say that? Those of us who have had the joy of sharing life with even just one of man's best friends certainly can attest to this!

Mine was a female chow-lab-shepherd mix named Dutch Girl that we adopted from the Lake City Animal Shelter on Christmas 1990 for our eleven-year-old daughter. Dutch was exceptional. She had the will of a bull, the intelligence of a child, and the devotion of Saint Paul to the Romans. She subverted a thief from entering our daughter's bedroom window; took on rattlesnakes; ran with the horses; chewed the bumper off the UPS man's truck; saved our daughter in the swimming pool; faced a skunk down—the only battle she ever lost; raised a baby rabbit; loved to run; ate ice cream; chased seagulls on the beach; loved mountain barbecue; and always showed us the utmost love and affection. Dutch had a life well lived and never let us down. There is no earthly price you can put on that!

Perhaps one of the most incredible animal miracles I have experienced came when Dutch was diagnosed with liver cancer in late October 2003, when she was fourteen years old. She had been losing her appetite and was having some small vomiting episodes with blood in the vomit. We quickly took her to the vet's office, where she was given tests and an MRI. We were told that her cancer was advanced, and that we could expect her to live only two to three more months at most.

The heart aches harder when it knows you are about to lose a beloved family member, especially at Christmas time.

It so happened that the traveling Image of Our Lady of Guadalupe was arriving in our diocese in December. It was going to be venerated in a Catholic church close to us, and I invited the guardian of the image to rest overnight at our home. To my surprise, she brought the image into our home, so we set it up in our living room.

Early the next morning, around 4:00 AM, I went into the living room with Dutch and prayed for Dutch's healing before Our Lady. I know it may sound presumptuous, but I believe that Mary, who is the Mother of the Lord of Creation, will come to our aid at such times as this. Who better to seek the Son's attention than his Mother? After praying, I walked Dutch to the front of the image and pressed her head against Mary's feet in the image. It was a very beautiful moment, and I felt better for having placed the Dutch Girl in Mary's hands.

By late January, we knew something was up! Dutch had been getting better, so we took her to the vet for an updated prognosis. It appeared that the cancer was in remission, and the vet was thrilled to see Dutch doing so well.

I believe it was a miracle. I believe that if you truly believe in the power of the unfathomable love that is given us by the Mother of God, who intercedes for us eternally with her Son, nothing is too small to ask for and nothing is impossible!

The cancer did recur in July, and we finally had to say good-bye. We were all better prepared at this point, having been given another six months of time to love Dutch and make more memories.

Our vet arrived around 11:00 AM on a hot Saturday that July, and Dutch, who would never allow anyone into our home without a resounding reception of loud barking, turned her head and wagged her tail. As our vet entered the house, she got up and went to him, placing her head in his hands. He couldn't believe how at peace she was and he sensed, as we did, that she wanted him to know that she *knew*, and she was thanking him. Believe me when I say that we were not humanizing this dog by her behavior; there was something very mysterious taking place, and we all felt it.

We thanked our doctor so much for coming, and asked for just a few moments to prepare to let her go. We gathered around Dutch, my husband, our daughter, and I, and we held her, telling her how much we all loved her. We offered a prayer in thanksgiving to God for her life and her love, and we blessed her with holy water. She looked at us with unbelievably peace-filled eyes, wagging her tail and lying quietly. She knew why the doctor was there, and she knew—as all animals know—that God was calling her. The needle was inserted, we hugged her, and then very quickly and quietly she fell asleep and left us.

I had seen my husband cry only two times before this moment, but Dutch's death was number three. We all cried, even our vet. After a while, we conducted her burial in the back of the house overlooking the lake where she had watched the wild ducks fly in. She was given to God's providence for safekeeping, because He holds all that He has created in His hands, destined to the glory He promises all creation through Jesus.

21

Miss Bunny Blueberry

It was a beautiful and sunny Thursday morning on Saint Augustine Beach, and I had the garden hose out on the back porch of our condo, watering some of my potted plants. In the peripheral vision of my left eye, I saw what I thought was a snake, and I heard a sharp peeping sound. Turning quickly, I saw a large five-to six-foot long tan coachwhip snake carrying a new baby bunny in its jaws, whipping through the high grass and heading right at me.

I took what I had, the garden hose, and I hit the snake's neck with the nozzle, causing the snake to drop the little rabbit into the tall grass at my feet. Both the snake and I went for the rabbit at the same time, and I got it! I dashed back to the patio, leaving the brazen snake to search again and again where the bunny had landed.

God smiled on that little bunny. She was no bigger than my thumb, with eyes shut tight and soft, tiny ears. I could see the alignment of heaven in the precise moment and the unusual way that the bunny had been saved. Just a harrowing split-second decision by me had rescued that little bunny, and I knew it wasn't by chance.

Bunny Blueberry—her new name—was a wild marsh rabbit, a very small brown rabbit indigenous to the beaches and marshes of north Florida. I had an obligation to try and help this little rabbit first to live, and then to return to its natural environment to live out its life.

I contacted a local wildlife rescue group for further help, thinking that maybe they had someone in place who could take the bunny. That was not to be the case, so I asked if they could advise me on trying to care for the rabbit myself. They gave me instructions prefaced with the words, "It is highly unusual for these infant rabbits to survive two weeks. But if it does, call us back, and we will help you further."

Well, sir, this little girl made it the two weeks. So we got the advanced course on raising her further from the rescue group. She would need to make it another two to three months before we could release her back into the wild.

As Bunny grew, it was evident that something was wrong with her hind legs. They seemed to be dragging to one side, and she would start to roll over after several hops. This was not good. It appeared that the snake might have pinched the nerves to one of her hind legs while it was carrying her, and now the possibility was surfacing that she would be a bunny with a disability.

Two months, then three months came and went, and my family and I decided we would just keep Bunny Blueberry. Our cat had already adopted her, and our dog was her biggest fan and guardian, so it was just meant to be. Bunny had us, and we would be her family—and we were for over five years. My husband said that the stock on a "national organic lettuce" company went way up after Bunny's arrival—not to mention how much she loved blueberries, thus earning her distinct title.

Bunny never could hop right. She learned to overcome her disability by hopping more on one hind leg, but if she tried to hop quickly, she would end up rolling over. Her leg never cooperated, and eventually it got to the point that it never moved.

Bunny let us know when it was her time to leave us. On December 12, 1998, I noticed that she was becoming lethargic and wouldn't eat. We went into preparation mode, which always requires prayer. I don't think I could make it without my prayer life, especially in dealing with death. As it was, Bunny made a miraculous recovery overnight and was her old self the next day.

Then December 27 arrived, and it was a different story. Bunny had been struggling more and more with eating and even with breathing. It was getting close. That morning, her eyes said it was time.

I took her around to the other animals to allow them to sniff her and, in their own unique way, to say good-bye, and I shared in Bunny's last moments with them. Then we blessed Bunny with holy water, prayed the prayer we called "The Reception Prayer" to Jesus, and my family and I petted her and loved her with kisses. Then I drove to my vet's office, having called ahead to make arrangements, and I prepared to be at her side for the moment of death.

Our vet is so compassionate; he handled her little body with such tenderness as she lay there, weak and dying. The injection was given, and Bunny Blueberry left peacefully. Our vet left me alone with Bunny for a little while so that I could make my final good-bye.

He returned eight or so minutes later to check her heart and to be sure that all was final. As he moved his stethoscope on her chest to confirm that she was no longer alive, her hind leg— the one that had never moved—began moving in a running motion. Now some might say it was just a muscle reflex, and perhaps it was. But my vet found it peculiar that the leg was not moving in a spasmodic way, but in a rhythmic, running motion.

For me it was a signal grace, a sign that having prayed for Bunny's safe return to her Creator, I received the grace to know I was heard. The little leg that never had been any good was now in the hands of God, and all was right with the world.

22

Bud, the Wonder Dog

At the beginning of this book, I wrote about taking Buddy Boy, my Dalmatian, with me on my trip to the mountains. Bud, like so many of my family's pet members, came to us in a way that only divine providence would allow.

My husband, Greg, and I were on our way to Sunday Mass one hot September day in 2006 when we noticed a rather large and energetic Dalmatian running for all he was worth in an open field a good distance away. It concerned us because it appeared that the dog was lost. We returned from Mass to find this very same dog lying on the side of the road in front of our home, suffering from heat exhaustion. Our home was over three-quarters of a mile away from where we had seen Bud running.

My husband looked up at the sky, closed his eyes, and said with surrender, "Lord, I give up."

It had always been an ongoing joke between Greg and I how animals would show up at our home. Greg would argue with me that it was somehow a secretive act on my part that got them there, with me making it look accidental. I always stood my ground and told him, "I did no such thing. It was God's doing!" Well, Buddy the Dalmatian helped put all that to rest!

Here Buddy was, lying weak and overheated, desperately in need of help. Greg and I got him up and to the front porch, where we administered cooling towels, cool water, and some food. It was a wonder he ended up at our home where we could help him, and we wondered where he came from.

There were two definitive signs about Buddy's past environment: his neck bore the stains of what must have been a tightly cinched leather collar, and his front feet had been wrapped in camouflage duct-tape.

I believe that Bud had freed himself from some restrictive tie down, choosing to run away and die, if that be the case, rather than to stay with his former owner any longer. Someone had definitely abused this beautiful animal, and he had had enough! It was a wonder he was able to get away ... or was it?

We kept Bud. He had never been neutered; he had some type of eczema; and he was diagnosed with heartworms. We doctored his skin disorder, had him neutered, and put him through the heartworm treatments. All of this was put into God's hands, and Bud the Wonder Dog survived with flying colors.

Bud was enthusiastic about everything! There was such joy in this great animal; how could anyone not love his sweet heart! Bud was athletic, energetic, and a first-class character that filled our days with the joy we had been missing since the loss of our Dutch Girl.

It was at this time that my husband was undergoing serious chemotherapy and radiation treatments for throat cancer. He and I both had missed Dutch Girl so much, and I truly believe the Lord sent Bud to us. Bud was my husband's constant companion during the painful months of treatments and hospital stays, watching Greg's every move and laying his head at my husband's feet while my husband napped. Greg had sworn he could never love another dog as much as he loved Dutch Girl, but he told me that Bud had won his heart all over again. At night Bud slept between the two of us, just like Dutch Girl used to do.

Then came the night before my dear Greg succumbed to the cancer. God was so good to me, having allowed the doctors to give me a final release to bring Greg home. Within twelve hours, Greg slipped into a coma.

The night before Greg died, Bud and my daughter's two dogs, Labrador mixes named Gator and Roxy, came into the room where Greg lay. We witnessed each of them sniff his hand and lick it, then lie down beside the bed. They remained there through most of the night. No one bothered them, and they chose to remain close to Greg. It was through their actions that I knew Greg was close to leaving us. They were holding vigil and saying good-bye.

After Greg passed away, Bud and I began our new journey together, both of us missing Greg terribly, but both of us supporting each other with love and long walks. Bud is a wonder dog to have survived abuse, a wonder dog to have survived heartworm treatments, a wonder dog to have gained my husband's heart and love, and he continues to be my wonder dog and best friend!

O heavenly Father, protect and bless all things that have breath; guard them from all evil, and let them sleep in peace.

—Albert Schweitzer[87]

23

Susi Meets Suzanne

I met Suzanne back in 1990. She was a beautiful green parrot with a love for children and most adults, especially Sister Marie Rene Azar from the order of the Sisters of Saint Joseph. This cute little bird was a gift to Sister Marie Rene from another nun, Sister Suzanne of the Sisters of the Visitation—a gift that came with a very studious character. Suzanne the parrot would ride in Sister's coat to visit the classrooms, and she kept an eye on Sister when Sister was in her office. It was a love affair that was just too sweet, and the kids loved it.

It was my privilege to serve Sister Marie Rene, our Catholic school principal, when I was president of the school's Parent-Teacher Organization.

It happened that a rather heated debate took place at one of the sixth-grade graduation meetings for parents. Another mother and I did not see eye-to-eye on the graduation activities. The debate took on the tone of an argument, and the topic was left tabled at an impasse.

Sister Rene had both of us come to her school office to discuss the matter further. After we were seated, Sister Rene walked quietly over to the parrot's perch from which the bird had been eyeing us. She motioned for Suzanne to move onto her finger. Turning, she brought Suzanne over and placed her on my left shoulder. Suzanne and I were eyeball to eyeball, and Suzanne was bobbing her head at me as if to say, "Stop being so hard to deal with!" The look in that parrot's eyes said that she meant it!

As we talked, I could feel the presence of that little parrot on my shoulder diffusing the tension in the room. I mean, what could look funnier than two women who really wanted to be mad at each other having to negotiate with a parrot standing in as mediator? The meeting ended with laughter and successful plans for the sixth grade's graduation.

When I handed Suzanne back to Sister Marie Rene, I said, "You're a real psychologist, aren't you? You knew this would happen!" to which she just smiled and winked.

Never underestimate the power of a little nun with a devoted parrot when it comes to handling tough situations. The healing power of the Holy Spirit certainly flows through all types of creatures as necessary!

Sister Marie Rene and I continue to share lunches together, and to this day we enjoy our talks about all of God's beautiful creation!

24

Josh and Jennifer Meet Mom and Dad

My father, Richard Kinney, retired from the insurance world in Miami and moved back to his father's estate in central Florida, settling down to grow oranges. He and my mother had a home that was like a little piece of heaven. It sat shrouded under towering oaks that dripped with Spanish moss, with two spring-fed lakes to either side of the property and wildlife at their back door.

Dad was out early one morning, making his rounds under the oaks with squirrel peanuts and bird food, when he noticed a fallen nest containing two small, featherless baby birds. It turned out that they were baby red-bellied woodpeckers. The parents, of course, wanted nothing to do with them, so Dad and Mom became surrogate parents. They were religious about feeding the babies, and kept them in a box with a down blanket in a warm corner of the kitchen. When the birds' eyes opened, Dad and Mom were the first creatures they saw, and of course they bonded as family immediately.

As Josh and Jennifer—their new given names— grew, they would peep for food, and then peep different peeps that said, "I'm full." They began to get fully feathered, and soon showed signs that they wanted to try out their flying ability. So Dad and Mom would take them outside at various times. Mom would hold them and Dad would call, and off they would fly to Dad, and vice versa.

The day came when they were ready to leave for good. So Dad and Mom drove out in the truck to the oak hammock, and said an emotional good-bye. Opening their hands, they let their babies fly off. Or so they thought.

As they drove back to the garage, Josh and Jennifer flew right in behind them. Out of the garage they all went, and a big, happy reunion took place. Dad and Mom spent some time with the birds, showing them where the bird feeders were, and they set up a makeshift home of branches and towels in the garage. Josh and Jennifer lived there a while longer.

In the mornings, when Dad and Mom would take their coffee strolls, Josh and Jennifer would fly along from tree to tree. When Dad would head out in the truck, Josh flew right outside the window. This went on for over a year, at which time Jennifer found a love. She and her love resided another six months on the property, but then moved on. Josh, however, stayed on until the end of his days. As he mated and had his own family, he became more the natural bird he was meant to be. He would come and visit Dad and Mom at first several times each day, but that dwindled to once a day.

The one tradition that never stopped was Dad going out in the evenings and calling out into the woods for Josh, and Josh always answering Dad with his loud *kwirr, kwirr, kwirr!* … and to all a good night!

As fate—or better yet, God—would have it, Josh's family and descendants continued to reside in the oak hammock. My daughter can remember years later being with her granddaddy and hearing him call to what she thought was Josh. My Dad told her that Josh had long since died, and he was calling Josh's grandson. Call it a fluke—or call it what we in our family believed it to be, a covenant of love—but this bird would answer my Dad in the evenings, just like his father and grandfather before him had done.

"Are not five sparrows sold for two pennies? And not one of them is forgotten before God."

—Luke 12:6

Part VI
Animals and Grief

25

Preparing Your Best Friend for Death

ooooooooooooooooooooooooooooooooooooooooo
For everything there is a season, and a time for every matter under heaven: a time to be born, and a time to die.... I know that whatever God does endures for ever; nothing can be added to it, nor anything taken from it; God has made it so.

—Ecclesiastes 3:1–2, 14

I want to preface this section with the truth that when death approaches, you must let God be God. Everything of this world is destined to a finite existence here, and all must go through the rite of passage, death, to move into the infinite. God's will is done in all things for those who believe in His omnipotence.

Death will come to your pet or animal friend, just as surely as it will come to you. It is something you can try and prepare for, but I have found it pretty hard to be prepared to let your loved one go. When it is imminent, each pet owner must approach the day of death as best she or he can. It is no easier to let go of a lifelong animal family member than it is to let go of a human family member. Sometimes, because our pets have shared so much of our personal lives with their unconditional love, it is harder to let the pet go.

You are the one who ultimately will decide how to handle the death of your beloved animal companion. Only you can make the decisions that accompany the death of a beloved family pet. I share my own personal experiences in hopes of offering comfort more than a guideline, though they can be that as well.

I must tell you in truth that the day your pet dies, things will never be the same—no more than it would be the same if you lost a relative. Each pet brings to a person's life a sense of beauty, wonder, and appreciation that only that pet, uniquely created by God, can bring. You must be able to accept the gift of your pet's life, and you must be a devoted steward who will cooperate with God when it is time to allow your pet to die, giving back to God the gift He shared with you. The joy of having and loving animals comes with knowing that one day you are going to have to let go.

Death could come like a thief in the night and your pet die suddenly or by accident; or you may have time to prepare for the moment. It may be from a natural cause or an unnatural cause, or you may have to make the decision to euthanize. No one way achieves any less pain in your heart than another in the process of your pet's death.

Knowing that you are about to lose your pet can cause a huge change in your priorities at the moment. It can be a time of reflection on a life well lived, perhaps a time to ponder the illness or injury that has caused the impending death, or a time of gentle healing. Sharing memories is a way to prepare for all concerned, and those can certainly be a source of comfort later on.

I have always had other pets at home when losing one of my animal companions. I do make it a priority, if possible, to allow them to say good-bye too. The animals can smell impending death; it is something that is given them by God, and they will sense your sadness. You would be amazed at how all my animals know what is happening, and how they respond with a nuzzle and a lick or a sniff, even a tap of the paw. Animals have that sixth sense that allows them to know so much more than we do.

If your pet has a partner, it will be harder for the partner when the pet leaves, as the pet left behind will grieve the loss like you do. Be alert to the needs of affection and consolation in the remaining pet or pets. They need to see you depart with your friend and theirs. You may notice that the remaining animal or animals in your home may exhibit sadness by seeming distant, not wanting to eat, even perhaps staying closer to you more than normal. They will share in your loss and will also be very in tune with your emotions—and why not? They are family. My gang of twelve pets has always been like my personal bereavement group. They are consoling companions that keep close company with me when we suffer the loss of a family pet member.

If you must choose to euthanize your pet, it all comes down to the timing. It can be an agonizing decision. You can selfishly wait too long and your pet may suffer needlessly; but act too quickly, and you may find yourself suffering from the sting of guilt.

How do I know it's the right time? I have found it is very important to have a prayer life at this time. You must offer up your concerns and tears to our Lord and ask for His guidance. All things come into the world through Him, and all things exit this world through Him. Just as the Lord knows when the sparrow falls, He will also concern Himself with the animal you love. Go to Jesus for consolation.

Your pet will let you know by the look in its eyes ... it is unmistakable. You will know it is time to euthanize because you have looked into those eyes a thousand times before. Your pet's eyes will communicate it to you, and you must be courageous enough to acknowledge it.

You must be attuned to signs in your discernment of your pet's situation. You are the one who knows your animal's routine and whether or not it is changing or has changed. You will know if your animal is in pain. You will witness its life functions start to shut down; this usually brings with it the need for you to care for your animal in a more intense and extraordinary way. You will know "the look" when your friend is ready.

Then it is up to you. You must decide how you want to handle your animal's humane euthanasia. There are decisions to be made by you in how you wish the procedure to go:

- Do you want to bring your pet to the veterinarian's office alone, or do you wish to bring other family members?
- Do you have a vet who will come and euthanize your pet at home if you prefer to have your pet pass away there?
- Would you rather a friend take your pet to the vet's office?

At the vet's office, your pet will be aware that there are those about who love it, and that they are there to help. I have witnessed this again and again with my animal family—the animal's loving submission to the veterinarian and the staff.

The pets I have had to euthanize because of a life-ending injury, old age, or a terminal medical condition have always shown great courage and love; it seems their inner self tells them that death is inevitable. They give me courage to face the moment with them. There have also been those that died quickly, without the option of going to the vet, and I have dealt with them at home in the same way that I have dealt with them at the vet's office. I am with them to the end; I embrace them with my arms and human love, handing them back in an unseen way to our Creator.

I have always supported the choice of the pet owner to be present in a last gesture of true friendship, to help his or her pet leave. It will be the hardest thing you will probably ever do, but your animal friend needs you to make the final release. When it is time for them to die, they really exhibit no fear; they want to go, and they know that you are present with them. In time, you will have the peace that comes from knowing you said good-bye.

If you cannot stay for the finality of the moment of death, please do take the time to speak with and love your pet before leaving or before someone takes the pet from you. This, too, will give you the peace of a loving release. I have been with and buried many of my forty-one lifetime friends, wild and domestic. They all have shown me great courage in death, as if they knew exactly the One who was calling them. I have never seen fear in the eyes of my animal brethren—only surrender, a willingness to move out of the pain they are in and into the hands of God.

We read in Romans:

> The creation itself will be set free from its bondage to decay and obtain the glorious liberty of the children of God. (Rom. 8:21)

I have always blessed my animal friends with holy water, then prayed a prayer of thanksgiving before letting them go. I value the power of holy water and use it in my home in ways supported by the teachings of the Church. I offer back to God, through Jesus, what has been and will be rightfully His. I thank Him for the presence of this beautiful creature in my life, for the time we had, and for the time to come.

You will have to take your own moment in handling the death of your beloved pet. It doesn't have to be vocalized; Jesus hears your innermost thoughts. You must do what you are capable of. But let Jesus help you!

Most every veterinarian I have dealt with who has put to sleep any one of my beloved friends has handled the moment with great reverence and gentleness. Now more than ever, veterinarians are extremely aware of pet owners' needs in the process of pet loss.

There is most often no pain in the euthanizing process. Veterinarians have special training in humanely euthanizing your pet. It is usually a two-step process. First, a sedative is given to calm your pet; next, the euthanizing injection gently stops the animal's heart, which is likened to going to sleep under anesthesia. There is no suffering!

Your pet will be aware as the needle is inserted and when the injections take place, and then it will just "fall into eternal slumber" as the heart slows and stops.

And lastly, how do you want to handle your pet's remains? There are options for pets just as there are for humans. There are pet cemeteries, your own back yard (if your county ordinance allows such), and cremation.

Having children in the home presents another situation, depending on the children's ages. You must be honest with them. Children are tremendously resilient and understand a lot more than they are sometimes given credit for. Do not tell them their pet went away or fell asleep, and the like. Do not tell them that the pet has become an angel; the angels are a separate creation apart from man and animals, with a different destiny in eternity with God. Do tell them that the pet is about to die, or has died. Tell them that God loves all He has created, *human and animal, and that He has a place for each and every one of us to come and live with Him.* Tell them their pet is in God's hands as we all are, and that God will take care of their friend. After all, He created this very special creature just for them. Share your sorrow, and allow your children to grieve. Faith leads us to the moment of death where we must allow God "to be God!" Trust in God! As we surrender what we love, we are cast into the bittersweet moment where we acknowledge

God's divine providence for our beloved animal companions, and we walk in faith.

Each person must move through the grieving process and the flood of memories that will fill his or her heart. If possible, discuss the death as a family. It is amazing the support and comfort that the people closest to you can give. But be prepared also for those who just want to be left alone. People must address their grief at their own pace and in their own unique ways.

26

Handling Your Grief

o o o o o o o o o o o o o o o o o o o o o o o o o o o o o o o o o o o o o o o
Even in laughter the heart is sad, and the end of joy is grief.

—Proverbs 14:13

To be able to reconcile yourself to the devastating loss of a much-loved animal family member, you must first face and withstand the pain of grief. Grief takes you to a "no-man's land" of emotional chaos that encompasses body, mind, and spirit. Anger, denial, guilt, and depression can reel about you like banshees. Call upon the strength and love of the Holy Spirit; Jesus pours out the Spirit to heal those who need healing. The book of Romans counsels:

> "Likewise the Spirit helps us in our weakness; for we do not know how to pray as we ought, but the Spirit himself intercedes for us with sighs too deep for words." (Rom. 8:26)

My first request of you is to *not* go out and adopt or purchase another animal companion right away. You will do both yourself and the animal a disservice. Let yourself feel the need for quiet reflection and a clearing of mind and heart to better love and give to a new animal family member. There also has to be a reconciliation to the loss. You and the Lord need time together, and you must allow time for the healing that only He can bring.

You are not alone in your pain of loss. Everything you are experiencing has also been experienced by Jesus. We are reminded of how Jesus wept for his friend Lazarus who had died. Jesus had a fully human heart and could feel the pain of separation. He grieved with Martha and Mary in the loss of Lazarus:

> When Jesus saw her weeping, and the Jews who came with her also weeping, he was deeply moved in spirit and troubled; and he said, "Where have you laid him?" They said to him, "Lord come and see." Jesus wept. (John 11:33–34)

There is great comfort in knowing that the Lord truly feels your pain and your loss. It is a time when you should run to His arms and allow Him to embrace you in your grief. He has the capacity to love you and comfort you as though you were the only person in the world.

Yet the sting of death, the emptiness you feel, is the start of what is called the *grieving process.* Grief is over, and yet at the same time, it continues on; grief must be lived. Each of us must grieve in our own unique way.

Your actions in the grieving process will more than likely dictate your recovery period. Do not rush yourself! There will be some days when nothing seems to help as pain grips you within. Other days you will be able to claim the pain and move in love to higher ground. You must understand that your sorrow cannot be ignored or abandoned, and you must trust yourself enough to claim it. You cannot wait for joy to once again return; you must go forward and find it. Insist on it! You cannot let death dominate the place of loss in your heart. It should never be allowed to take away that place where your lost loved one lives.

Healing will only begin when you are able to acknowledge your true feelings. Acknowledging your pain helps to loosen the hold that the pain has on you. Jesus knew that, so He allowed himself to weep for His friend. Open your channel of communication with Jesus, who understands and has planned and provided for your sorrow. Even if you are angry, let Him know it. He can handle your anger, and will love you all the more. There is no timeframe for the conclusion of a grieving period. You must be patient with yourself and move to accept that it takes as long as it takes.

"Behold, I make all things new!" (Rev. 21:5). That is the promise of Jesus. Take a stand in the peaceful inheritance that is promised to you and all of creation by a God who wills only that you choose to share eternity with Him—an eternity where not even our earthly attachments can be lost! God's divine providence continues to preserve all that is and has been created from nothing.

When we ourselves pass from this life and stand before Jesus, who is all truth and all justice; when all is revealed to us, who among us would dare utter, "You are wrong, Lord!"? The joy we experienced on earth will be brought to an eternal fullness. All that was important to us on earth, all that we loved, all that brought us great joy—you can bet that the Father, the Son, and the Holy Spirit know it intimately. God promises a renewal for all of creation, whose very existence echoes the essence of love Himself!

The greatness of God's love is the power that will see "all that was created good" to its ultimate reward!

Finis

Therefore from the beginning I have been convinced, and have thought this out and left it in writing: The works of the Lord are all good, and he will supply every need in its hour. And no one can say, "This is worse than that," for all things will prove good in their season. So now sing praise with all your heart and voice, and bless the name of the Lord.

—Sirach 39:32–35

27

Greg and Mary:
The Final Chapter

o o o o o o o o o o o o o o o o o o o o o o o o o o o o o o o o o o o o o
For what can be known about God is plain to them, because God
has shown it to them. Ever since the creation of the world his
invisible nature, namely, his eternal power and deity, has been
clearly perceived in the things that have been made.

—Romans 1:19–20

I am just ready to send this book to the publisher when an event so
unexplainable happens that I must stop to include it.

The passing of my husband Greg nine months earlier has left the
family with a huge hole in our hearts; but no one is affected as much
as Mary, his cat!

Now Greg didn't pick Mary; he was never one to fancy one cat
in the house more than another. However, when Mary entered our
life—abandoned and hungry—on the feast day of Mary, January 1,
2001, she chose Greg as The One. He was the sun that rose in the east,
and all things hoped for. The two of them had a wonderful love affair
of special pets and privileged seating arrangements. Greg allowed Mary
to sit with him on his lap—unlike the other cats, which were relegated
to sitting at his feet.

Greg's passing caused Mary to become depressed. We noticed it
about the third month he was gone. It had gotten to the point where
she seemed ill, so I took her to the vet's office. After some blood tests
and diagnostics, it was determined that nothing appeared wrong. Yet
she continued to lose weight and seemed to be moving into frail health.

Several trips later proved that she indeed had problems with her left ear. Using steroids and antibiotics, we hoped to ward off whatever it might be. Then fluid and blood started to flow from the ear. She was taken to an animal neurologist for help.

A scope revealed that Mary had squamous cell carcinoma of the middle ear that was aggressively advancing into the left side of her neck and head. She was not going to be able to live much longer.

I was in shock as the doctor told me the diagnosis. I asked him, "Is this common in cats?"

He answered, "Not really—it's most uncommon."

Greg's cancer battle had been against advanced squamous cell carcinoma in the left larynx and hypopharynx; it had metastasized into the left side of his head and also into the lymph nodes in the left side of his neck.

The vet was stunned. He asked me if Greg had ever smoked.

I answered, "Yes, all of his life."

I knew where he was going with this, so I continued, "Doctor, he always smoked on the back porch, and Mary would never sit with him when he was smoking—she didn't like it."

All either of us could do was shake our heads. It was just beyond coincidence. In fact, it was too coincidental for words, as it speaks powerfully to the realm of what we don't understand in the ties between human and animal. For me personally, there is the overwhelming spirit of divine providence and a sign of grace in love.

Throughout that weekend, I carried Mary out to the back porch and sat with her in the evenings, both of us enjoying the fall breeze and the beautiful sunsets. She would rest on the ottoman until dark. Our other pets exhibited an unspoken knowledge of Mary's condition, each one taking a special interest in her, nosing her, licking her, or just lying close by.

Tuesday morning, Mary and I visited all of our pet family together for one final good-bye before we left for the animal clinic. Once there, we entered through the rear door, where we were escorted to a quiet room in the back.

Mary would leave this world right here, her quality of life gone. She was ready.

I sat at her side just as I had done with Greg for the two years he had fought the cancer. At the end, I held Greg's hand and cradled his head, and now I cradled Mary's head and stroked her neck. I have always been there for all my family when God calls. And why shouldn't I be there? God asks each of us to take that walk sooner or later, and some of us must make the walk with others before it is our time to go. Understand that it is a calling from God that you are given the task of seeing those you love off to eternal rest. Walk with God on this, and He will use you as an instrument of peace.

Mary purred so loudly that even the doctor was taken aback by it. Her purrs were, I am sure, grateful acknowledgements and thank-yous for the love that surrounded her in that room.

I spoke to her, telling her how much she was loved and that she was just a breath away from being with the one she loved most, her sweet Greg. I choked back tears as I said, "And I am envious of what your eyes will behold, and how you will be held." (I must confess here that I have always held close to my heart the hope that our pets see God immediately.) I am ever plagued with feeling weak when I cry. Jesus cried at the tomb of Lazarus, (John 11:35) and Saint Francis of Assisi wept over the body of a dog killed during a war. [88]

We prayed over Mary, preparing her for the final release. As the injection was given, her purrs began to fade, and I could feel her slipping away. Within a minute she was gone, with only eternity there to separate me from Mary and Greg.

I brought Mary home, and her remains have a beautiful spot in the east yard facing the corner garden, where we have a statue of the Blessed Mother, and where Greg loved to sit.

At the end of a long night of sleeplessness or suffering, sunrise brings joy and hope for the day to come. At the end of the long night of death and sin, the rising of Christ, the Sun of Justice, brings joy and hope for the life to come. In the light of the resurrection, we see and live anew, knowing that all is in and from God's hand, returning all to him with thanks and praise.

—The Magnificat[89]

Part VII
A Call to Action

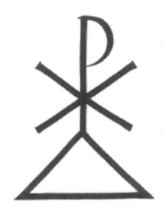

28

Catholic Stewards of Creation

o o o o o o o o o o o o o o o o o o o o o o o o o o o o o o o o o o o o
For he has made known to us in all wisdom and insight the mystery of his will, according to his purpose which he set forth in Christ as a plan for the fulness of time, to unite all things in him, things in heaven and things on earth.

—Ephesians 1:9–10

We are called by our Creator to be co-operators with Him in His plan for the stewardship of creation. As creatures of God's creation, we are to embrace our surroundings as members of the family of creation. This chapter is a "call to action" for all Catholics to reflect on their personal responsibility toward creation and the environment. I find that the devil beats us up by keeping us busy. We can busy ourselves, about ourselves, for ourselves, and leave Christian stewardship out on the periphery of important things in our lives.

By making a personal commitment to become a Catholic steward of creation, you are answering the call to step up your day-to-day living, to become a cooperator with Jesus in the plan of redemption for all the earth, to join in a more harmonious way with the Creator-God who has given you the great and generous gift of all creation.

A Web site created by this author and dedicated to this very premise is available at **www.catholicstewardsofcreation.com.** Here you can find numerous opportunities to become involved in responsible stewardship in your specific area of the country. The site offers articles, guest columnists, books, tips, a pet memorial, a "share"space, blogs, parish resources, and products. It also features links to a multitude of Catholic and governmental web sites and news sites that are concerned with ecological and environmental issues, including climate change; animal issues; marine life; the cosmos; gardening and agriculture; self-help initiatives; and more to aid you in your desire to serve God in better stewardship of creation.

The booklet, *Renewing the Earth,* available from the United States Conference of Catholic Bishops (www.usccb.org), is a wonderful tool for the Catholic faithful to start with in their journey to better stewardship of the planet. It gives an overview of the Church's teaching and invites the faithful into love for God's creation, a respect for nature, and a commitment to practices that bring these attitudes into their daily life.

The Catholic Stewards of Creation web site would like to address that commissioning at a grassroots level by bringing the faithful to a "rally site" where they can move forward and be inspired to greater actions of creation stewardship.

Catholic families should be the world's frontrunners in seeing to it that laws and institutions support and defend all life from the womb to the tomb, and that there are sanctions to protect creation and the natural environment. We all can play a part, whether it's supporting those agencies that deal locally or worldwide with animals that are in abusive or abandoned situations; starting a Community Sponsored Agriculture (CSA) project for your parish, neighborhood, or city; supporting your state's legislation against capricious actions against the land; protecting turtle nesting areas on our coastlines; joining the new movement, Catholic Coalition on Climate Change; or writing world leaders regarding global environmental dangers.

We must take back the dignity given to our humanity as stewards and respond to the original ministry given us in the Garden of Eden: to care for this world with the same providential care God intended! We must support and strengthen a culture of reverence for *all* life that God has created—human, animal, vegetable, or mineral!

Future generations will either be thanking us or condemning us for what is passed on to them in the world they will live in.

> Man's dominion over inanimate and other living beings granted by the Creator is not absolute; it is limited by concern for the quality of life of his neighbor, including generations to come; it requires a religious respect for the integrity of creation.[90]

We must strive to keep the sense of fraternity with all of God's creatures and the created world. We are not only obliged but, as stewards, we are charged with the ministry and care of creation.

God loved us first, and He will love us last. In all that God has done for us since the Garden of Eden, I am sure that as we ascend in our love for Him, He will bring to fullness the love for those we hold dear in our hearts—and that includes all that we have loved on earth. We are all the family of creation!

"I came that they might have life, and have it abundantly."

—John 10:10

Helpful Web Sites

American Animal Hospital Association
http://www.aahanet.org

American Catholic
http://www.americancatholic.org

American Society for the Prevention of Cruelty to Animals
http://www.aspca.org

American Veterinary Medical Association
http://www.avma.com

Arbor Day Foundation
http://www.arborday.org

Audubon Society
http://www.audubon.org

Catholic Coalition on Climate Change
http://www.catholicsandclimatechange.org

Catholic Conservation Center
http://conservation.catholic.org

Catholic Online
http://www.catholiconline.com

Catholic Stewards of Creation
http://www.catholicstewardsofcreation.com

Franciscans International
http://www.franciscansinternational.org

Humane Society of the United States
http://www.hsus.org

Just Faith Ministries
http://www.justfaith.org

L'Osservatore Romano
http://www.vatican.va/news_services/or/or_eng/index.html

Lost or Missing Pets
http://www.missingpetpartnership.org

National Parks Conservation Association
http://www.npca.org

National Wildlife Federation
http://www.nwf.org

United States Conference of Catholic Bishops
http://www.usccb.org

Vatican
http://www.vatican.va

World Society for the Protection of Animals
http://www.wspa-us.org
http://www.wspa-international.org

Recommended Literature

Armstrong, Dave. *A Biblical Defense of Catholicism*. Manchester, NH: Sophia Institute Press, 2003.

Murray Bodo. *Francis: The Journey and the Dream*. Cincinnati, OH: St. Anthony Messenger Press, 1988.

Brown, Rev. Eugene M. *Dreams, Visions & Prophecies of Don Bosco*. New Rochelle, NY: Don Bosco Publications, 1986.

Brown, Michael H. *The Other Side*. Palm Coast, FL: Spirit Daily Publishing, 2008.

Frio, Ilis, O.S.F.; Warner, Keith Douglass; Wood, Pamela. *Care for Creation: A Franciscan Spirituality of the Earth*. Cincinnati, OH: St. Anthony Messenger Press, 2009.

John Paul II. *Crossing the Threshold of Hope*. New York, NY: Alfred A. Knopf, Inc., 1994.

Johnson, Timothy J. *Bonaventure: Mystic of God's Word*. Hyde Park, NY: New City Press, 1999.

Johnson, Timothy J. *The Soul in Ascent*. Quincy, IL: Franciscan Press, 2000.

Keller, Phillip W. *Lessons from a Sheepdog*. Nashville, TN: W. Publishing Group, 1983.

MacNutt, Francis, PhD *Healing*. Notre Dame, IN: Ave Maria Press, 2006.

Murphy, Charles M. *At Home on Earth: Foundations for a Catholic Ethic of the Environment*. New York, NY: The Crossroad Publishing Company, 1989.

Order of the Friars Minor, Province of the Most Holy Name. *The Francis Book*. New York, NY: Macmillan Publishing Co., Inc., 1980.

Perego, Jeanne. *Joseph and Chico: The Life of Pope Benedict XVI as Told by a Cat*. San Francisco, CA: Ignatius Press, 2007.

Ratzinger, Cardinal Joseph; Seewald, Peter. *God and the World: A Conversation with Peter Seewald*. San Francisco, CA: Ignatius Press, 2000.

Ripley, Canon Francis. *This is The Faith: A Complete Explanation of the Catholic Faith*. Rockford, IL: Tan Books and Publishers, Inc., 2002.

Roberts, Monty. *The Man Who Listens to Horses*. New York, NY: Ballantine Publishing Group, 1996.

Senior, Donald. *The Catholic Study Bible: The New American Bible Including the Revised New Testament*. Oxford, UK: Oxford University Press, Inc., 1990.

Endnotes

Declaration

1. *Catechism of the Catholic Church,* 2nd ed., paragraph 890.

Introduction

2. Catholic Encyclopedia. *Providence, Divine*: Kevin Knight, 2008. http://www.newadvent.org/cathen/p.htm.

Chapter 1

3. John Bartlett, *Familiar Quotations* (Secaucus, NJ: Citadel Press, 1998).
4. St. Thomas Aquinas. *Summa Theologica: Complete English Edition in Five Volumes,* Translated by the Fathers of the English Dominican Province. (New York: Benziger Bros., 1948)
5. Pope John Paul, II. *Crossing the Threshold of Hope.* (New York: Alfred A. Knopf, Inc., 1994).
6. Maryann Mott, "Pets Enjoy the Healing Power of Music." *LiveScience.com.* http://www.livescience.com/animals/080103-harp-therapy.html.
7. Phillip W. Keller, *Lessons From a Sheepdog* (Waco, TX: Word Books, 1983).
8. Monty Roberts, *The Man Who Listens to Horses* (New York: Random House, 1996, 1997).
9. Sandy Robins, "The Pope and the Pussycats." *MSNBC. com.* http://www.msnbc.com/id/8219384/print/1/displaymode/1098.
10. Michael H. Brown, *After Life* (Goleta, CA: Queenship Publishing Company, 1997). Betty J. Eadie, *Embraced by*

the Light (Detroit, MI: Gold Leaf Press, 1994). Michael H. Brown, *The Other Side* (Palm Coast, FL: Spirit Daily Publishing, 2008).

11. Raymond A. Moody Jr., *Life After Life* (San Francisco: Harper Collins, 1975).

12. Raymond A. Moody Jr., *Life After Life* (San Francisco: Harper Collins, 1975). Betty J. Eadie, *Embraced by the Light* (Canada: Bantam, 1994). Michael H. Brown, *The Other Side* (Palm Coast, FL: Spirit Daily Publishing, 208).

13. P. M. H. Atwater, *The New Children and Near Death Experiences* (Rochester, NY: Bear & Company, 2003). Dr. George G. Ritchie, *Return from Tomorrow* (Grand Rapids, MI: Baker Publishing Group, 1995). Raymond A. Moody, Jr., *Life After Life* (San Francisco: Harper Collins, 1975). Rev. Eugene M. Brown, *Dreams, Visions & Prophecies of Don Bosco* (New Rochelle, NY: Don Bosco Publications, 1986). Robert C. Broderick, *Heaven the Undiscovered Country* (Huntington, IN: Our Sunday Visitor, 1990).

14. Dr. George G. Ritchie, *Return from Tomorrow* (Grand Rapids, MI: Baker Publishing Group, 1995). P.M.H. Atwater, *Coming Back to Lfe: The After-Effects of the Near Death Experience* (Secaucus: Citadel Press, 2001). Michael H.Brown, *The Other Side* (Palm Coast: Spirit Daily Publishing, 208)

15. Dr. Howard Storm, *My Descent into Death* (New York: Doubleday Religious Publishing, 2005). Ned Dougherty, *Fast Lane to Heaven* (Charlottesville, VA: Hampton Road Publishing Company, 2001). Father Martin von Cochem, O.S.F.C. *The Four Last Things* (New York: Benziger Brothers, 1900). Peter J. Kreeft, *Every Thing You Ever Wanted To Know About Heaven* (San Francisco: Ignatius Press, 1990). Peter J. Kreeft, *Angels and Demons:What Do We Really Know about Them?* (San Francisco: Ignatius Press, 1995).

16. Dr. Howard Storm, *My Descent into Death* (New York: Doubleday Religious Publishing, 2005). Ned Dougherty, *Fast Lane to Heaven* (Charlottesville, VA: Hampton Road Publishing Company, 2001).

17. Rev. Eugene M. Brown, *Dreams Visions & Prophecies of Don Bosco* (New Rochelle, NY: Don Bosco Publications, 1986).

18. Zuzic, Dr. Marco. *A Short History of St. John in Ephesus* (Lima, OH: The American Society of Ephesus, 1960).

Chapter 2

19. Nietzsche, Friedrich Nietzsche, *The Antichrist,* section 16, Quotations by Author, www.quotationspage.com/quotes/ Friedrich_Nietzsche/31.

20. Friedrich Nietzsche, "Twilight of the Idols." *Handprint. com.* Translated by Walter Kaufmann and R.J. Hollingdale. http://www.handprint.com/SC/NIE/GotDamer.html.

21. Aleister Crowley, "True Will." *The Book of the Law Liber AL vel Legis sub figura CCXX.* http://www.hermetic.com/ crowley/engccxx.html.

22. Pontifical Council for Culture, Pontifical Council for Interreligious Dialogue. "Jesus Christ the Water Bearer of Life: A Christian Reflection on the 'New Age.'" *Vatican Information Service,* Vatican City. http://www.vatican.va/ roman_curia/pontifical_councils/interelg/documents/rc_ pc_interelg_doc_20030203_new-age_en.html.

23. Pope Benedict, XVI. "John Scotus Erigena." *Libreria Editrice Vaticana.* General Audience addressed June 10, 2009. http:// www.vatican.va/holy_father/benedict_xvi/audiences/2009/ documentshf_benxvi_aud_20090610_en.html.

Chapter 3

24. Thomas Nicol "The Old Latin Version (International Standard Bible Encyclopedia)." *Bible-Researcher.com.* http://www.bible-researcher.com/oldlatin.html.

25. *Catechism of the Catholic Church,* 2nd ed., paragraph 282.

26. *Catechism of the Catholic Church*, 2nd ed., paragraph 287 (Cf. *Isa* 43:1; *Ps* 11:15; 124:8; 134:3.
27. *Catechism of the Catholic Church*, 2nd ed., paragraph 302.
28. *Catechism of the Catholic Church*, 2nd ed., paragraph 1043 (*2 Pet* 3:13; cf. *Rev* 21:1; *Eph* 1:10).
29. *Catechism of the Catholic Church*, 2nd ed., paragraph 1047 (St. Irenaeus, *Adv. Haeres.* 5, 32, 1:PG 7/2, 210).
30. *Catechism of the Catholic Church*, 2nd ed., paragraph 1048 (GS 39 *S* 1.).
31. *New Saint Joseph Sunday Missal and Hymnal.* Complete Edition. Rev. John C. Kersten, S.V.D.(New York: Catholic Book Publishing Co.,1986).
32. *Catechism of the Catholic Church*, 2nd ed., paragraph 314 (1 Cor. 13:12).
33. *Catechism of the Catholic Church*, 2nd ed., paragraph 2415 (Cf. *CA* 37-38).
34. *Catechism of the Catholic Church*, 2nd ed., paragraph 2416 (Cf. *Mt* 6:26; *Dan* 3:79-81).
35. *The Catholic Study Bible*, The New American Bible. (New York: Oxford University Press, 1990).

Chapter 4
36. *Catechism of the Catholic Church, Second Edition*, paragraph 667.

Chapter 5
37. *Catechism of the Catholic Church, Second Edition*, paragraph 280 (*GCD* 51).
38. *Catechism of the Catholic Church, Second Edition*, paragraph 342 (Cf. *Ps* 145:9).
39. *Catechism of the Catholic Church, Second Edition*, paragraph 353
40. Pope John Paul, II. "God Made Man the Steward of Creation." *L'Osservatore Romano.* Weekly Edition in English, 24 January 2001, 11.

Chapter 6

41. *Catechism of the Catholic Church*, 2nd. ed., paragraph 354.
42. *Catechism of the Catholic Church*, 2nd. ed., paragraph 288(Cf. *Gen* 15:5; *Jer* 33:19-26).

Chapter 7

43. *Catechism of the Catholic Church*, 2nd. ed., paragraph 391 (Cf. *Jn* 8:44; *Rev* 12:9; Lateran Council IV (1215): D*S* 800).
44. Johnson, Timothy J. *The Soul in Ascent* (Quincy: Franciscan Press, 2000).

Chapter 8

45. *Catechism of the Catholic Church*, 2nd. ed., paragraph 1701 (Cf. *GS* 22).
46. Bodo, Murray. *Francis, The Journey and the Dream* (Cincinnati: St. Anthony Messenger Press, 1988).
47. *Catechism of the Catholic Church*, 2nd. ed., paragraph 668 (*Eph* 1:10; cf. *Eph* 4:10; *1 Cor* 1:24, 27-28).

Chapter 9

48. *Catechism of the Catholic Church*, 2nd. ed., paragraph 376 (Cf. Gen 2:17; 3:16; Cf. Gen 2:25).

Chapter 10

49. *Catechism of the Catholic Church*, 2nd. ed., paragraph 703 (Byzantine liturgy, Sundays of the second mode, *Troparion* of Morning Prayer).
50. *Catechism of the Catholic Church*, 2nd. ed., paragraph 41 (*Wis* 13:5).
51. M. Maher and J. Bolland. (1912). Soul. The Catholic Encyclopedia. New York: Robert Appleton Company. New Advent: http://www.newadvent.org/cathen/14153a.htm.

52. *Catechism of the Catholic Church*, 2nd. ed., paragraph 366 (Cf. Pius XII, Humani Generis: DS 3896; Paul VI, *CPG S* 8: Lateran Council V (1513): DS 1440).

Chapter 11
53. St. Thomas Aquinas. *Summa Theologica: Complete English Edition in Five Volumes* (New York,: Benziger Bros., 1948).

Chapter 12
54. Charles E. Rice *50 Questions on the Natural Law* (SanFrancisco: Ignatius Press, 1999).
55. Marian Stamp Dawkins. *Animal Minds and Aimal Emotions* (Oxford, UK: The Society for Integrative and Comparative Biology, 2009).
56. *Catechism of the Catholic Church*, 2nd. ed., paragraph 314 (*1 Cor* 13:12; Cf. *Gen* 2:2).
57. YouTube: Dog Risks Life to Save another Dog. http://www.youtube.com/watch?v=DgjyhKN_35g.
58. Julianna Kettlewell. BBC News science reporter. *Farm Animals Need Emotional TLC.* http://newsvote.bbc.co.uk/mpapps/pagetools/print/news.bbc.co.uk/1/hi/sci/tech/4360947.stm.

Chapter 13
59. Roy M. Gasnick *The Francis Book* (New York: MacMillan Publishing Co., Inc., 1980).
60. *Wolf of Gubbio,* Wikipedia, http://en.wikipedia.org/wiki/Wolf_of_Gubbio). Murray Bodo, *Francis: The Journey and the Dream* (Cincinnati: St. Anthony Messenger Press, 1988). Julien Green, *God's Own Fool: The Life and Times of Francis of Assisi* (San Francisco: Harper Collins Publisher, 1985).
61. William P. Thayer. *Gubbio-Monument to Saint Francis and the Wolf.* http://penelope.uchicago.edu/Thayer/E/Gazetteer/

Places/Europe/Italy/Umbria/Perugia/Gubbio/Gubbio/
Wolf_Monument.html.

Chapter 14

62. E. Marsh (1912). The Salesian Society. In The Catholic
    Encyclopedia. New York: Robert Appleton Company. New
    Advent: http://www.newadvent.org/cathen/13398b.htm.
    Lives of Saints (New York: John J. Crawley & Co., Inc.,
    1954). Wikipedia. http://en.wikipedia.org/wiki/Saint_
    John_Bosco.

63. F. A. Forbes, *Saint John Bosco* (Rockford, IL: Tan Books
    and Publishers, Inc., 2001). Father Paul O'Sullivan. An
    Excerpt on beliefnet.com. *Angel Dog. http://www.beliefnet.
    com/Inspiration/Angels/2000/08/Angel-Dog.aspx. John Bosco.*
    Bacchiarello, Father J. Bacchiarello, SDB, *Forty Dreams of
    St. John Bosco* (Rockford, IL: Tan Books and Publishers,
    Inc., 1996.

64. Patrick Lanagan, *Salesians: Don Bosco.* http://www.
    catholicfounders.org/donbosco.htm.

Chapter 15

65. N. Dal-Gal (1907). St. Anthony of Padua. In The Catholic
    Encyclopedia. New York: Robert Appleton Company.
    New Advent: http://www.newadvent.org/cathen/01556a.
    htm. Joan Carroll Cruz, *Mysteries Marvels Miracles in the
    Lives of the Saints* (Rockford, IL: Tan Books and Publishers,
    Inc.,1997). *Preaching to the Fish,* Saint Anthony of Padua.
    2009 PPFMC Messaggero di S.Antonio Editrice net
    http://www.saintanthonyofpadua.net/portale/santantonio/
    miracoli/santo/mirac3.asp.

66. *Saint Anthony of Padua, Part 2.* Catholic Exchange. http://
    catholicexchange.com/2006/06/30/83233. Saint Anthony
    of Padua. 2009 PPFMC Messaggero di S.Antonio
    Editrice net http://www.saintanthonyofpadua.net/portale/
    santantonio/miracoli/santo/mirac2.asp

67. *Saint Anthony and the Real Presence.* Catholic-Pages. http://www.catholic-pages.com/mass/corpus.asp. *The Mule* Saint Anthony of Padua. 2009 PPFMC Messaggero di S.Antonio Editrice net http://www.saintanthonyofpadua.net/portale/santantonio/miracoli/santo/mirac2.asp. Stoddard, Charles Warren Stoddard, *St. Anthony The Wonder Worker of Padua.* Rockford, IL: Tan Books and Publishers, Inc., 2nd ed. 1971)

68. *The Mule* Saint Anthony of Padua. 2009 PPFMC Messaggero di S.Antonio Editrice net http://www.saintanthonyofpadua.net/portale/santantonio/miracoli/santo/mirac2.asp.

Chapter 16

69. C. Mulcahy, (1909). *St. Germaine Cousin,* Catholic Encyclopedia. New York: Robert Appleton Company. New Advent: http://www.newadvent.org/cathen/06474a.htm.

70. C. Mulcahy, (1909). *St. Germaine Cousin,* Catholic Encyclopedia. New York: Robert Appleton Company.New Advent: http://www.newadvent.org/cathen/06474a.htm.

71. *Saint Germaine Cousin.* Wikipedia. http://en.wikipedia.org/wiki/Saint_Germaine_Cousin. Michael Michael, *Butler's Lives of the Saints* (Kent: Burns & Oates Limited, 1991).

72. *Saint Germaine Cousin.* Wikipedia. http://en.wikipedia.org/wiki/Saint_Germaine_Cousin. Michael Walsh, *Butler's Lives of the Saints* (Kent: Burns & Oates Limited, 1991).

73. C. Mulcahy, (1909). *St. Germaine Cousin,* Catholic Encyclopedia. New York: Robert Appleton Company.New Advent: http://www.newadvent.org/cathen/06474a.htm.

Chapter 17

74. St. Rochus Parish, Johnstown, PA. *Life of Saint Rochus.* http://webpages.charter.net/strochus/liferoch.html. *The Story of Saint Rocco.* San Rocco Culture Committee. http://www.sanrocco.org/story_of_saint_rocco.php. G. Cleary, (1912). *St. Roch.* Catholic Encyclopedia. New York: Robert

Appleton Company. New Advent: http://www.newadvent.org/cathen/13100c.htm.

75. Wikipedia. *Saint Roch,* http://en.wikipedia.org/wiki/Saint_Roch.

76. Wikipedia. *Saint Roch,* http://en.wikipedia.org/wiki/Saint_Roch. *St. Roch Patron Saint of Dogs & those who love them.* Saints Preserved. *Saint Roch.* http://www.saintspreserved.com/roch/roch.htm. G. Cleary, (1912). *St. Roch.* In The Catholic Encyclopedia. New York: Robert Appleton Company.New Advent: http://www.newadvent.org/cathen/13100c.htm.

77. Cleary, G. (1912). *St. Roch.* In The Catholic Encyclopedia. New York: Robert Appleton Company.New Advent: http://www.newadvent.org/cathen/13100c.htm. *The Story of Saint Rocco.* San Rocco Culture Committee. http://www.sanrocco.org/story_of_saint_rocco.php.

78. Wikipedia. *Saint Roch,* http://en.wikipedia.org/wiki/Saint_Roch.

Chapter 18

79. Wikipedia. *Rita of Cascia.* http://en.wikipedia.org/wiki/Saint_Rita_of_Cascia. *St. Rita.* Catholic Tradition. http://www.catholictradition.org/Cascia/rita1-2.htm#BIRTH. Joan Carroll Cruz, *Mysteries Marvels Miracles in the Lives of the Saints.* (Rockford, IL: Tan Books and Publishers, Inc., 1997).

80. *St. Rita.* Catholic Tradition. http://www.catholictradition.org/Cascia/rita1-2.htm#BIRTH. Joan Carroll Cruz, *Mysteries Marvels Miracles In The Lives of the Saints.* (Rockford: Tan Books and Publishers, Inc., 1997).

81. *St. Rita.* Catholic Tradition. http://www.catholictradition.org/Cascia/rita1-2.htm#BIRTH. Joan Carroll Cruz, *Mysteries Marvels Miracles in the Lives of the Saints.* (Rockford, IL: Tan Books and Publishers, Inc., 1997).

82. Wikipedia. *Rita of Cascia*. http://en.wikipedia.org/wiki/ Saint_Rita_of_Cascia. Joan Carroll Cruz, *Mysteries Marvels Miracles in the Lives of the Saints*. (Rockford, IL: Tan Books and Publishers, Inc., 1997).

Chapter 19

83. A. Astrain, (1909). *St. Francis Xavier*. Catholic Encyclopedia. New York: Robert Appleton Company. New Advent: http:// www.newadvent.org/cathen/06233b.htm. *Little Pictorial Lives of the Saints*. (New York: Benziger Bros., 1925).

84. Cristina Osswald, *A Saint and His Image: Francis Xavier*. Company Magazine,2003 http://www.companysj.com/ v202/xavier.htm. Joan Carroll Cruz, *Mysteries Marvels Miracles In The Lives of the Saints*. (Rockford, IL: Tan Books and Publishers, Inc., 1997) Melaka Tourism. *In Honour of Malacca's Saint*. http:/www.tourism-melaka.com/St_ FrancisXavier.html.

85. Cristina Osswald, *A Saint and His Image: Francis Xavier*. Company Magazine, 2003 http://www.companysj.com/ v202/xavier.htm. Joan Carroll Cruz, *Mysteries Marvels Miracles in the Lives of the Saints*. (Rockford: Tan Books and Publishers, Inc., 1997).

86. *The Jesuit Gourmet: The Crab, The Cross and St. Francis Xavier*. May 6, 2006, http://thejesuitgourmet.blogspot. com/2006/05/crab-cross-and-st-francis-xavier.html. Melaka Tourism. *In Honour of Malacca's Saint*. http:/www. tourism-melaka.com/St_FrancisXavier.html.

Chapter 22

87. Albert Schweitzer, *Essential Writings*, in press. The Albert Schweitzer Fellowship. http://www.schweitzerfellowship. org.

Chapter 27
88. Roy M. Gasnick, *The Francis Book* (New York: MacMillan Publishing Co., Inc., 1980).
89. Pierre-Marie Dumont, *Magnificat,* October 2008 Issue, page 184.

Chapter 28
90. *Catechism of the Catholic Church,* 2nd ed., paragraph 2415 (Cf. *CA* 37-38).

Sources and References

Arminjon, Father Charles. *The End of the Present World and the Mysteries of the Future Life.* Manchester, NH: Sophia Institute Press, 2008.

Astrain, A. "St. Francis Xavier." *The Catholic Encyclopedia.* New York, NY: Robert Appleton Company, 1909. http://www.newadvent. org/cathen/06233b.htm.

Bartlett, John. *Familiar Quotations.* Secaucus, NJ: Citadel Press, 1998.

Bodo, Murray. *Francis: The Journey and the Dream.* Cincinnati, OH: St. Anthony Messenger Press, 1988.

Book of Blessings. Washington DC International Committee on English in the Liturgy, Inc., Liturgical Press, Order, nn. 949, 1987.

Broderick, Robert C. *Heaven the Undiscovered Country.* Huntington, IN: Our Sunday Visitor, Inc., 1990.

Brown, Michael H. *After Life.* Goleta, CA: Queenship Publishing Company, 1997.

Brown, Michael H. *The Other Side.* Palm Coast, FL: Spirit Daily Publishing, 2008.

Brown, Reverend Eugene M. *Dreams, Visions & Prophecies of Don Bosco.* New Rochelle, NY: Don Bosco Publications, 1986.

Catechism of the Catholic Church. 2d ed. Washington DC: United States Catholic Conference, Inc.—Libreria Editrice Vaticana, 1997.

Companion to the Catechism. San Francisco, CA: Ignatius Press, 1995.

Crowley, Aleister. "True Will." *The Book of the Law Liber AL vel Legis sub figura CCXX.* http://www.hermetic.com/crowley/engccxx. html.

Cruz, Joan Carroll. *Mysteries Marvels Miracles in the Lives of the Saints.* Rockford, IL: Tan Books and Publishers, Inc., 1997.

Dawkins, Marian Stamp. "Animal Minds and Animal Emotions." *Integrative and Comparative Biology* 40 (2009): 883–88.

Dougherty, Ned. *Fast Lane to Heaven.* Charlottesville, VA: Hampton Roads Publishing Company, Inc., 2001.

Dumont, Pierre-Marie, ed. *Magnificat.* Yonkers, NY: Magnificat USA LLC. 10 (October 2008).

Eadie, Betty J. *Embraced by the Light.* Detroit, MI: Gold Leaf Press, 1994.

Father Delaporte of the Society of Mercy. *The Devil: Does He Exist and What Does He Do?* Rockford, IL: Tan Books and Publishers, Inc., 1982.

Forbes, F. A. *Saint John Bosco.* Rockford, IL: Tan Books and Publishers, Inc., 2001.

Green, Julien. *God's Fool: The Life and Times of Francis of Assisi.* San Francisco, CA: Harper Collins Publisher, 1985.

Gasnick, Roy M. *The Francis Book.* New York, NY: Macmillan Publishing Co., Inc., 1980.

Timothy J. Johnson *The Soul in Ascent: Bonaventure on Poverty, Prayer, and Union With God.* Quincy University: Franciscan Press, 2000.

Harris, Trudy, R.N. *Glimpses of Heaven.* Grand Rapids, MI: Revell, a Division of Baker Publishing Group, 2008.

Keller, Phillip W. *Lessons From a Sheepdog.* Waco, TX: Word Books Publisher, 1983.

Kettlewell, Julianna. "Farm Animals 'Need Emotional TLC.'" *BBC News.* http://newsvote.bbc.co.uk/ mpapps/pagetools/print/ news. bbc.co.uk/1/hi/ sci/tech/ 4360947.stm.

"Life of Saint Rochus." *Saint Rochus Parish.* http://webpages.charter. net/strochus/liferoch.html.

Kreeft, Peter. *Every Thing You Ever Wanted To Know About Heaven . . . But Never Dreamed of Asking.* San Francisco, CA: Ignatius Press, 1990.

Lewis, C. S. *The Problem of Pain.* London: Collins, 1940.

Latin-English Booklet Missal for Praying the Traditional Mass. 3rd ed. Glenview, IL: Coalition in Support of Ecclesia Dei, 1995.

Laux, Father John, M.A. *Chief Truths of the Faith.* Rockford, IL: Tan Books and Publishers, Inc., 1990.

Linzey, Andrew and Tom Regan, eds. *Animals and Christianity: A Book of Readings.* London: SPCK and New York: Crossroad, 1989.

LiveScience.com. "Pets Enjoy the Healing Power of Music." *Today. MSNBC.com.* http://today.msnbc.com/id/22539914.

McInerny, Ralph. *Thomas Aquinas Selected Writing.* London: Penguin Books, 1998.

Moody, Raymond A. Jr., M.D. *Life After Life.* 2nd ed. San Francisco, CA: Harper San Francisco, 2001.

Mott, Maryann. "Pets Enjoy the Healing Power of Music." *LiveScience.com*. http://www.livescience.com/animals/080103-harp-therapy.html.

Kersten, Reverend John C., S.V.D. *New Saint Joseph Sunday Missal and Hymnal*. Complete Edition. New York: Catholic Book Publishing Co., 1986.

Nicol, Thomas. "The Old Latin Version (International Standard Bible Encyclopedia)." *Bible-Researcher.com*. http://www.bible-researcher.com/oldlatin.html.

Nietzsche, Friedrich. "The Antichrist." *Quotations by Author*. www.quotationspage.com/quotes/Friedrich_Nietzsche/31.

Nietzsche, Friedrich. "Twilight of the Idols." *Handprint.com*. Translated by Walter Kaufmann and R.J. Hollingdale. http://www.handprint.com/SC/NIE/GotDamer.html.

Penaskovic, Richard. "The Mule and the Fish." *Messenger of St. Anthony*. http://www.messengersaintanthony.com/messaggero/pagina_articolo.asp?IDX=239IDRX=72.

Pope Benedict XVI. "John Scotus Erigena." *Libreria Editrice Vaticana*. General Audience addressed June 10, 2009. http://www.vatican.va/holy_father/benedict_xvi/ audiences/2009/documentshf_ben-xvi_aud_20090610_en.html.

———, "Pope Benedict XVI's Prayer Intentions for August." *Libreria Editrice Vaticana*. http://www.vatican.va.

Pope John Paul II. "Apostolic Letter Tertio Millennio Adveniente of His Holiness Pope John Paul II to the Bishops, Clergy and Lay Faithful on Preparation for the Jubilee of the Year 2000." *Libreria Editrice Vaticana*. http://www.vatican.va/holy_father/john_paul_ii/apost_letters/ documents/ hf_jp-ii_apl_10111994_tertio-millennio-adveniente_en.html (November 10, 1994).

————, *Crossing the Threshold of Hope*. New York, NY: Alfred A. Knopf, Inc., 1994.

————, "Divine Providence Continues to Care for Creation." *Libreria Editrice Vaticana*. http://www.vatican.va/holy_father/john_paul_ii/audiences/1986/documents/hf_jp-ii_aud_ 19860507_sp.html.

————, "God Made Man the Steward of Creation." *L'Osservatore Romano*. Weekly Edition in English, 24 January 2001, 11.

————, "God Will Judge the World with Justice." *Libreria Editrice Vaticana*. http://www.ewtn.com/library/PAPALDOC/JP951119.HTM.

————, "The Holy Spirit Acts in All Creation and History". Holy Father's General Audience Address of August 12, 1998. *Catholic Conservation Center*. http://conservation.catholic.org/holy_spirit_acts_in_all_creation.htm.

————, "Mary and the Redemption of Creation." *Vatican Information Service*, Vatican City. Liturgy of the Word celebrated in Zamosc, Poland on June 12, 1999. http://conservation.catholic.org/pope_john_paul_ii.htm.

————, "New Era Brought by Christ." *Vatican Information Service*, Vatican City. General Audience addressed February 14, 2001. http://conservation.catholic.org/ pope_john_paul_ii,_page_4.htm.

————, "Peace with God the Creator, Peace with All of Creation." *The Ecological Crisis a Common Responsibility: Message of His Holiness for the celebration of the WORLD DAY OF PEACE January 1, 1990*. http://www.ewtn.com/library/PAPALDOC/JP900101.htm.

Pontifical Council for Culture, Pontifical Council for Interreligious Dialogue. "Jesus Christ the Water Bearer of Life: A Christian Reflection on the 'New Age.'" *Vatican Information Service*, Vatican City. http://www.vatican.va/roman_curia/pontifical_councils/

interelg/documents/   rc_pc_interelg_doc_20030203_new-age_
en.html.

Ritchie, Dr. George G. *Return from Tomorrow.* Grand Rapids, MI:
Baker Publishing Group, 1995.

Roberts, Monty. *The Who Listens to Horses.* New York, NY: Ballantine
Publishing Group, 1997.

Robins, Sandy. "The Pope and the Pussycats." *MSNBC.com.* http://
www.msnbc.com/ id/8219384/print/1/displaymode/1098.

Saint Augustine. "Sermons 241: Easter: c.411 A.D." Vatican
Information Service, Vatican City. http://www.vatican.va/ spirit/
documents/spirit_20000721_agostino_en.html.

Saint Gregory of Nyssa, *The Lord's Prayer and The Beatitudes.* Mahwah,
NJ: Ancient Christian Writers, Paulist Press, 1978.

Saint Thomas Aquinas. *Summa Theologica: Complete English Edition in
Five Volumes.* New York,: Benziger Bros., 1948.

Seewald, Peter. *God and the World.* Translated by Henry Taylor. San
Francisco: Ignatius Press, 2002.

Socias, Reverend James, ed. *Daily Roman Missal.* 4th ed. Illinois:
Midwest Theological Forum, Inc., 1998.

Storm, Dr. Howard. *My Descent into Death.* New York, NY: Doubleday
Religious Publishing, 2005.

Thorold, Algar. *The Dialogue of the Seraphic Virgin, Catherine of Siena*
Rockford, IL: Tan Books and Publishers, Inc., 1974.

United States Census Bureau, Year 2000.

Vann, Rev. Joseph, O.F.M. *Lives of Saints.* New York, NY: John J.
Crawley & Co., Inc., 1954.

Walsh, Michael. *Butler's Lives of the Saints.* Rockford, IL: Tan Books and Publishers, Inc., 1997.

Williams, Rev. Thomas David. *A Textual Concordance of the Holy Scriptures.* Rockford, IL: Tan Books and Publishers, Inc., 1985.

Zuzic, Dr. Marko. *A Short History of St. John in Ephesus.* Lima, OH: The American Society of Ephesus, 1960.